JUAN THE LANDLESS

JUAN THE LANDLESS
JUAN GOYTISOLO

REVISED EDITION TRANSLATED BY PETER BUSH

DALKEY ARCHIVE PRESS ⑤ CHAMPAIGN & LONDON

Originally published in Spanish as *Juan sin tierra* by Editorial Seix Barral, 1975
Copyright © Juan Goytisolo, 1975
Revised edition and Afterword © Juan Goytisolo, 2006
Translation copyright © Peter Bush, 2009
First Dalkey Archive edition, 2009

Library of Congress Cataloging-in-Publication Data

Goytisolo, Juan.
  [Juan sin tierra. English]
  Juan the landless / Juan Goytisolo ; translated by Peter Bush. -- Rev. ed.
    p. cm.
  ISBN 978-1-56478-527-5 (pbk. : alk. paper)
  I. Bush, Peter R., 1946- II. Title.
  PQ6613.O79J7813 2009
  863'.64--dc22
                        2008051423

Partially funded by grants from the National Endowment for the Arts, a federal
agency; the Illinois Arts Council, a state agency; and by the University of Illinois at
Urbana-Champaign.

This publication was partly supported by a grant from the Program for Cultural
Cooperation between Spain's Ministry of Culture and United States Universities.

This work has been published with a subsidy from the Directorate-General of Books,
Archives and Libraries of the Spanish Ministry of Culture.

www.dalkeyarchive.com

Cover: design by Danielle Dutton, illustration by Nicholas Motte
Printed on permanent/durable acid-free paper and bound in the
United States of America

The face distanced itself from the ass.

Octavio Paz, *Conjunctions and Disjunctions*

I'm completely dead to decency.

T. E. Lawrence, *Letters*

*Word against fact, guerrilla against traditional warfare,
incantatory affirmation against objectivity and,
generally speaking, sign against thing.*

Jacques Berque, *Les Arabes*

I

according to the gurus of Hindustan, at the highest stage of meditation, purged of appetites and longings, the human body joyfully
surrenders to an ethereal existence, all passions and ailments shed,
attentive only to the listless flow of time without end, light on the
wing like those meandering little birds seemingly inspired by the
gentle melodies of an invisible breeze, musically absorbed in distant contemplation of the sea : sensual stimuli and thrills no longer take their toll and, immersed in the righteous languor of an
eternal present, the human body loftily disdains derisory enslave-
ment to pleasure, pure and slender, subtle and weightless, beneath
a delicate flow of twilight clouds that usher in majestic autumnal
landscapes far from the frenzy of the madding crowd : rising above
the tyranny of miserable contingency to offer the devout marvel-
ing populace an ascetic's severe serenity honed by penitence and
fasts, the aloofness of a Brahmin martyr cheerfully confronting
the preparations for his own death, the grave fakir lying calm and
graceful on his bed of nails : but the body gazing at you from a corner of the table, from that garish LP cover, evidently in violent pro-
test, almost screaming, will never, no never, in the unlikely event
the idea has ever entered its head, accede to the highest stage of
transcendental meditation, the austere albeit ineffable joys of the
holy life of contemplation : neither anchorite nor fakir nor Brahmin : pure body : matter in motion : child of the earth and tied to
the earth : rather than tight clean lines, rigidly confined surfaces,
spare austerity, ostentatious displays of rotundity and curve, festi-

val of flesh, baroque splendor : opulent and fertile, generous and succulent, firmly rooted in the nether world by virtue of its feet, outside the sleeve's artistic frame, but by all accounts rivaling everything else in their grandeur, prodigality and excess : unshod, naturally, seeking the direct symbiotic contact that extracts the vital impulse, genitive powers from the primeval substance : the rich sap that nourishes and gives life, selflessly helps it thrive, invents magnificent convexities : the dipping neckline's oppressive rim strains to contain them and triggers off a huge rush of waves, that, though hidden by stretchy velveteen, still tempt the eyes of the alert onlooker : from the commanding flowing chin-line down, erect turbid surfaces unleash furious eddies anticipating full-frontal apotheosis : a twin-crested tsunami the fearful Caribbean cyclone has catapulted to incredibly dizzying heights : the lethal wave rearing up horrendous magnificent moments before crashing on the disaster zone sweeping away with wrathful precision homes, chattels, settlements, industries, crops in an area brimming with life, transforming it in the blink of an eye into a sad desolate quagmire, the preserve of wailing victims, barking dogs, hovering vultures, pillaged by looters and the starving and the rushed last-minute zeal of fleur-de-lis'd international do-gooders : but the wave advances no further, collapses and the photographer's snapshot calms, assuages and stills : the corsage's Maginot Line suggests rather the hypothesis of two ovaloid tumescent hillocks, their distant salients trapped in precarious unlikely equilibrium : mountain ranges, riverbeds, hills, passes, ravines? : no : geometry gives us a better route in : circles, disks, spheres, orbs that invite study and scrutiny, the discerning speculations of a land surveyor dreaming of sole ownership of the sumptuous grandeur of this spectacular semicircle : and

2

doesn't the goddamned woman know it too, an arrogant broad smile on her open voracious fleshy lips : simultaneously extending her huge arms, lewdly inciting a stranger to penetrate the arcane sites of earthly paradise : carefully permed hair, smooth bulging forehead, bushy eyebrows, broad flat nose, large gleaming white teeth, pink flickering tongue, dark tanned skin : two gold-plated earrings dangling, apparently jangling sweetly while she gleefully guarachas to the bilingual legend on the LP sleeve : THE QUEEN OF RHYTHM, LA REINA DEL RITMO : a right royal body respecting no law but her own sovereign pleasure : rising proudly above experiences of detachment from self and meditation : resolutely partial to a very precise hic and nunc : a here and now situated beneath the undulating folds of the flowery dress she flourishes and flaunts in a whirlwind of laughter, letting all comers know that she, the fat lady, aspires only to give and take pleasure because life is juicy and must be squeezed dry without qualms or theories, crudely but acutely aware that there is no other reality beyond what you see, fancy and touch, that there is no such thing as a sweet tamarind or immaculate mulatta : her cyclopean mass is silhouetted against the blurry buildings of a sugar-mill and, making a detour around her, you step inside : the faded tobacco-colored photos that presided over the conclave of ghosts from your childhood aren't here to light your way and probably still adorn the walls of the old mansion in that country whose name you would rather not remember : severed moorings, withered roots, scant supporting material : scattered over the table, on the board over the brass sink, across the shelves of a ridiculous and shabby filing cabinet, the explosive fat lady's Seeco Record brings an extravagant touch of color and relegates the remaining props to the back of your memory : the soft greenish covers of the book with the engraving that explains the various numbered parts of a typical vacuum evaporator : the photocopy of a spine-chilling "Exposition of Christian Doctrine Suited to the Mentality of Docile Blacks" : images, that is, from those not-so-distant dead and abolished times when the rebellion let its hair grow long and its hurricane of hope shook the stunted existences of millions and millions of beings sentenced over centuries to the ideological servitude that comes with your language, dazzling you all with a spectacle of violent unpolished beauty, before your tribe's age-old predisposition to suppress the vibrant freedoms of today in the name of the imaginary freedoms of tomorrow subordinated creative invention to the imperatives of production, sacrificed nation to plantation and once more crushed its children like cane in the mill, restoring Fidelity Island to its loathed perennial condition as a one-sugar-crop landed estate : no other element in the room could accompany your steps down the arduous path of your return to the gene, to the sin of the origins they oppressed you with : and adrift in the vast expanse of the refinery, back turned on the fat rumbera, you must still appeal to the faltering, almost moribund glimmer of those antique pictures while you wander like a shade, past press and drying shed, warehouses and purging room : down the twists and turns of memory, in search of the slave huts : long before your aborted birth a century or so ago, invisible and ubiquitous now, but liberated from the stigma of skin color, ever ready to embody and begin the cycle anew

take a good look : their faces will seem familiar : the overseer has gathered them in front of the master's mansion and the clanging bell summons wretched stragglers from the canebrake to a privileged live view of the portentous event : the tropical sun blisters down on their heads and they protect themselves as best they can with brightly colored handkerchiefs and rustic palm-frond hats : assembled separately, the females fan themselves, gesturing femininely, ever flirtatious in spite of the dust, filth and their threadbare clothes : deputy-overseers and boundary guards patrol at the back with their whips and dogs and house slaves add the final touches to the dais draped in brocades and carpets where when the time comes, the clean righteous family will most probably sit : you pause for a few seconds to sketch in the details : sofas, rocking chairs, hammocks, a grand piano for their musical daughter, bowls of ferns, baskets of fruit, bouquets of flowers : the oval portrait of a domineering great-grandmother presides over the festive ceremony, a mulatto boy with angel wings fends off flies with a yarey palm frond : the other elements appear in the descriptions of customs from the era of Cecilia Valdés and the insistent harassing clang of the bell spares you from any need to linger : a tray of cold drinks, a delightful book of poetry, a Beethoven score, a bottle of West Indian rum? : the director's thoughtful staging will focus the eminently respectable intruder's attention on the empty double throne, erected on the damascened pedestal and protected from the sun by an airy canopy, also clearly awaiting the sovereign presence that like the pyx within the gold of the monstrance immediately provides the raison d'être, its magical resplendence filling it to the brim with august power : a liturgical symbol the mere existence of which stuns and fulminates, subdues and enslaves : relief and solace alike to pontifical and regal buttocks, endowed here with a satin cushion whose lovely embroidered hems conceal from the dismal rabble the secrets of a circular double cavity, sheltered by the throne's brocaded sides, beneath which, looking on, waiting respectfully, impatiently, is the sublime sublimating device, beloved child of puritan prurience, last fling of the mighty English industrial revolution : placed expressly so its virtual occupants from the exalted summit of their glory can gaze down upon the humble trench that, within reach of their sight but not their smell, readies itself to receive offerings from twenty-odd individuals of both sexes specially selected by the overseer's beady eye : a meter apart, following the strict norms of barracks discipline, squatting down and offering the fraternal assembly those jovial round-faced parts certain naturist photographers liked to record for the delectation of those so inclined, in the act of rivaling, in happy unison, Aeolus's ruddy cheeks : artfully playing their varied panoply of wind instruments : flutes, fifes and flageolets, oboes, clarinets and saxophones : obeying the baton of the snapshot's Mr. Anonymous with the expert timing of musicians performing an overture as the ladies sigh in their proscenium boxes and a devotee of bel canto in the stalls follows the score by the light of a miniscule torch, as proud and tiny as a firefly : but the picture postcard, in all its lyrical effusion, only half captures the juicy scene you're trying to conjure up : the dark bass harmonies of the hurrays, that's right, a thousand hurrays for those blessèd behinds peering at you and the humble resigned multitude as if they wanted to take your picture and laugh at you the way you laugh at them, with the sudden nervousness of someone splitting their sides and releasing long repressed tension via a short sharp breaking of wind : the ribaldry is mutual and, after the glorious enlightenment, after depositing their stools, the jocund donors proceed to eliminate the traces of their spontaneous euphoria with the minimal movement of a hand wiping away the remains of a smile : with a bucket for a washbasin : under the reproachful gaze of the family that meanwhile will have taken possession of the podium : great-grandfather Agustín and his wife, the young master, the girls, a group of poor worthy relatives, the household slaves, a fussy band of wet-nurses : little Adelaida plays the violin and an inspired young Master Jorge melodramatically thuds the ivories, little Fermina revises her chapter of French, the chaplain recites his matins, the little mulatto absorbed in his cameo role as a cherub tirelessly fends off flies : the overseer drinks rum from the bottle and cracks his whip over black heads as the trial run is about to begin : the engineers of the company that patented the contraption are trying to hide their nerves behind an elegant veneer of British phlegm and, hand in hand, with the pomp of monarchs about to be crowned, great-grandfather and wife ascend the steps of the throne accompanied by a religious silence : he wears white from head to foot, and sports a double-breasted jacket, gold chain and glowing Havana cigar : she looks identical to the faded portrait that watched over your anxious footsteps down the long passageway in that gloomy mansion : better still : in the ceremonial uniform of the Peninsula's Patron Virgin when receiving the honors from the Captain-General on the Day of the Hispanic Race : diamond tiara, sky-blue ermine-edged cloak and a royal scepter she grips aggressively as if someone had tried to snatch it away and she wanted to show the world her bellicose, nay thuggish readiness to defend it : scowling like that other distinguished monarch who perpetually crushed stubborn sects and swore not to change her undershirt till the infidels' presence profaned no more the fatherland's sacred sod : solemn and hieratic next to the handsome figure of the plantation owner : enveloped, like him, in the cloud of fine incense that seems to issue from the tip of his cigar : heady and pure, fragrant as balsam : a timely backdrop to the concerted efforts required by the demonstration : the non-material invisible odorless perfect emission that, thanks to the rear flaps conceived by the astute family tailor, plummets down the double cavity to the central cistern, that vault of riches immaculate and aseptic as a bank's : hidden likewise from the envious glances of those who merely trade their sweat for the burnished stuff, and never hoard it or get rich : de-surplus-valued blacks of the common trench, in direct contact with coarse matter, vile relief, viscerally plebeian emanations : the English engineers hover over their invention, try to gauge from the tension or relief on the protagonists' faces the success or failure of the prophylactic operation : the creature's fathers, when all's said and done, they rush and leap around the dais, their manicured hands behind them, their red heads overwrought : desperate to reach the end of the trial run : hanging on the pronouncement of the doctor in the adjacent room, performing an arduous stressful caesarean : while the slave holding bates its breath, the chaplain prays and the crowd of domestics stays silent and still : the suspense augurs a grandiose event and great-grandmother gradually erases her scowl and bows her forehead in approval : the diaphanous epiphany of a woman who can see her efforts truly crowned and feel her heart swelling at the subtle sweetness of the reward : she exchanges tender knowing glances with her husband, pulls the chain hidden inside the canopy and, closing her eyes in mystical rapture, mutters almost to herself

I shat like a queen

and though nobody will catch the mistress's message, a thousand fantastic rumors immediately spread across the plantation and the niggers will remain anxious and confused, peering in vain at her moving lips, unable to understand, down to their jungle mentality and scant notions of technology and theology, the celebrations of those who begat the creature, the new steam-engine, the wonderful water closet, now dancing for joy, tossing sweets to the children, hugging and congratulating them, while great-grandfather silently greets this luminous victory for the science of concealment, this sublime feat of engineering that further distances animal from human being, slave from sugarocrat, and, anticipating events by virtue of the holy powers his post confers, the plantation's stipendiary chaplain will go down on bended knee, intone the verses of the Magnificat and, eyes awash with tears, proclaim ecstatically to the four winds that Rome has declared, after duly considering the quantity and quality of the evidence provided, that the act they have all just witnessed must be accepted beyond any shadow of a doubt, any opinion voiced to the contrary being evidence of heresy, punishable by ecclesiastical tribunal and subject to relaxation by the secular arm, as a one hundred per cent genuine miracle

a miracle, yessiree, a miracle : or perhaps those crappy shit-faced niggers think the Son of God and the White Virgin and the saints and all the blessèd in Heaven defecated during their earthly lives into stinking trenches and dried their nefast eyes on grass and cobs of sweet-corn? : the idea would be absurd if it weren't already blasphemous : for while God's Eye radiates light and whiteness, the anus of the beast, the devil's eye, oozes disease and stench, filth and sin : their functions are mutually exclusive and opposed : as angelic St. Thomas of Aquinas says : what is partially corrupted is corruptible in its entirety and such a scenario would be abhorrent and sacrilegious even to the most hardline of heretics : this much is clear, very clear : neither Our Redeemer nor the Virgin expelled fecal matter : anyone who wanted to defend such a specious lie would be unable to find a scrap of evidence : let them revisit the Gospels, the Acts of the Apostles, the manuscripts of the Fathers of the Church, to no avail : simple common sense says it all : visceral discharges, be they solid or liquid, and all other bodily excretions, such as hair, sweat, nails, saliva and mucous, would, had they ever existed, necessarily partake of the Son's divine nature or the Mother's supernaturally privileged status and, imbued with an immutable eternal substance, would have been lovingly preserved by pious souls as priceless holy relics : however, as the said relics are nowhere to be seen and we find no mention of them in the revealed texts or patristic writings or works of the saints, we must conclude, consensus omnium, nemine discrepante, that they never existed and that Our Redeemer and the Virgin were not subject to the animal necessities that afflict men and force them to recoil shamefully from the act of restoring to the earth, in such a base unclean manner, what they took from it in the guise of delicious tidbits and refreshing cordials, for it is here that the whole divine bowel-evacuation hypothesis is exposed in its patent absurdity : it is common knowledge that animals and humans are patently inferior to plants and trees in one regard : the latter's superfluities are delightful and lovely, while those of bipeds and quadrupeds nauseate and disgust and if the former attract and please us with the aromas and flavors of their fruits, pray tell me : who but the devil could relish the sordid and horrible products of animal and human innards : here lies the heart of the matter : who will dare argue that Our Redeemer and the Virgin are inferior to the vegetable species? : any three-year old would indignantly reject such nonsense! : of course, the smart-asses among you will ask : well, didn't Our Redeemer and the Virgin eat? : the Gospels teach us quite the contrary : so tell us, father : what happened to the dishes they consumed if they didn't excrete them : oh, ye men of little faith! : I was coming to that! : if the metabolism of the vegetable kingdom differs from those of animals and humans, what's so strange about the Son of God's and his exalted Mother's also being different? : while the devil's eye secretes putrefaction and impurity, our Lord's exhales harmony and fragrance : simply compare the volume and shape of your rear ends with those on sacred statues and images and confirm their diverse functions at a glance : on the one hand, the compact light ethereal lines of exquisitely decorative ornamental organs : on the other, lewd rude curves proclaiming a base connection with obscene matter : oh, if only we could see the sweet-smiling mother-of-pearl Eye the Virgin hides beneath her sky-blue cloak, glittering with gold and precious stones! : only the blessèd enjoy that privilege and only God delights in its gracious beauty : even the most enraptured expressions of the mystics couldn't hope to describe and do justice to such prodigious perfection : a second, a fraction of a second, would allow you to appreciate the difference : the abyss separating her Charm from your disaster : the salacious anus, the black sewer down which you pour your dung, detritus and diarrhea : from which the devil speaks and the reason why you linger in filthy defecation and shamelessly surrender to the vice of sodomy : but not everybody's the same : fortunately, classes still exist : and Our Lord, in His infinite wisdom, has ordained that creatures on earth rise above the animal state and its impure secretions in order and rank according to merit :

some open their nefast eyes over the steaming miasmas rising off the public trench : others gradually purify themselves in elegant secluded lavatories : until they attain the ideal of the saints and the blessèd in Paradise, whose residues, St. Bernard tells us, are transformed into a refined mild liquid, similar to frankincense and myrrh : God, through his Divine Mediatrix, raises his creatures step-by-step to the highest level of fragrance and today He rewards the services of this holy devout family that gives food and shelter to so many many slaves by letting it clamber a step further up the steep stairs leading from stench to scent, from quadruped to angel and demonstrates His mercy to the world via a simple and edifying miracle : the act of evacuation without sound or fury, in a noble aseptic manner : you and I are witness to this act : let us bless the Lord and give Him our thanks!

what kind of music do they play in Heaven? : Bach, Handel, Mozart, Beethoven? : sonatas, lieder, operas, symphonies? : the reports you have at hand are scrappy and quite unreliable, though the cheeky playful attitude of the cherubim reproduced in colored prints in the pious books from your childhood betray a hint or at least a relative inclination, nay, a weakness for Italian music : those tuneful catchy airs today used in news broadcasts to provide the backing for a hectic cycling championship : when chorus and orchestra energetically fling themselves into the main theme in hot pursuit of the first violin : modulating arpeggios and trills, tremolos and staccatos that transport the audience rapturously to a theatrical paradise : up in the gods at La Scala, the very cusp of musical theogony! : unless, impelled by her obscure military calling to dally with the watch, the Lieutenant Nun on the Captain of the Fleet's

Vessel requests a potpourri of jigs and operettas : nothing warrants such a hypothesis, so you should admit your complete ignorance on the subject : Rossini, Chapí or Brahms : what difference does it make? : in any case, the Deo Gratias the chaplain intones will provide a short jubilant antiphon : pleasing, of course, to our Maker's ear : but unlikely to get a rise out of that fat stick of dynamite about to burst out of her shiny record sleeve : pushing her huge bust forward, a cetacean fretting and shaking, like jelly : rivalling that other camp diva, roaring like a wild beast over her grand piano's solemn black ivories : ready to demand the tasty fruit that led to our common father's expulsion from paradise : the glossy sheen of the eternal apple all ready for nibbles and fake blushes : or, better still, a banana : a tropical pineapple : a suggestive pear : greedily opening her huge lips : drooling like Pavlov's dog : wanting it whole : erupting like a wild volcano : torrents of lava, fumaroles, deflagrations : endless, Etnically orgasmic howls the orchestra extends with delirious intensity : and the example spreads with sibylline logic : not waiting for any Latinate antiphon, the blacks swathe their necks and waists in gaudy scarves rumba and guaracha inciting the females, with their beckoning hands, open palms and teasing thumbs touching bulky crotches: the women spring to their feet, swing and shimmy their parts : the mill-yard turns dance floor, bedecked and decorated as if for a St. John's Night party : the fat lady stretches her powerful arms, embraces the entire holding, takes it into her unlikely patronage and family and servants immediately abandon the platform with its piano, chairs, throne and water-closet : the chaplain will speak

we took your females away to deny you the opportunity to sin and to increase your output, but, stubborn in your depravity, you clung to your vices : your evil is too deeply ingrained and clearly incurable : nonetheless, how beautiful it would have been to see innocent white souls humbly disguised by black unworthy skin! : chaste and diligent, above vile pleasuring, mindful of God and his Son's supreme sacrifice : for the good shepherd sees all and watches your behavior like a zealous overseer : the Heavenly Master's prayers would have urged you on and his stewards and servants applauded your gentleness and piety, the treasure that is your humility, resignation and affection : black you may be, but you have the potential to be honorable : and to help you triumph in your efforts we bolted and padlocked the huts of your females : precisely to prevent them from inciting you to fornicate, with the frailty that is the mark of women of your species : we tried to ensure you didn't cohabit and indulge in venal harmful copulation : but your devious nature overcame our meticulous precautions : and behind our backs you continued to procreate, turning out these despicable measly children, dark-featured and from diseased stock : never stopping to think of the time pregnancy steals from your master and the expense rearing a nigger brood entails : the poor man, always burdened by your problems! : and then you complain that Don Agustín isn't happy : how can you expect him to be if you behave like that! : sins and yet more sins : because you'll do it anywhere : in the canebrake, next to the press, in the runs : I know all about it, I have my informants : your cigars always hanging out, pointing at your negresses as soon as our backs are turned : and they show what they've got as well : act as if they're pissing, opening wide, revealing all! : but the other gentle kind Overseer watching from Above finally loses his rag : not satisfied with offending his eyes with your dirty color, squat noses and thick lips :

to boot you blacken your souls by sinning dreadfully : Our Father in his hammock, in the Heavenly ancestral house, is curious to know what the holding is doing, and so he asks the White Virgin : what are those Lequeitio niggers in Cruces up to, the slaves belonging to the Mendiola and Montalvo Company? : are they behaving themselves? : are they obedient? : do they meet their quotas? : redeem their sins through work? : and the Mistress, poor thing, what does she see? : well, what you were doing right then : gawping at your females spreading their legs and defecating, negresses urinating, buttocks held high! : and you lot unbuttoned too, proudly flaunting your sooty imps : and she watches you play with them, finger them and engage in all sorts of filth : and the Father, in his hammock, lights his Havana and resumes his round of questions : are they respectful? : are they humble? : are they good? : do they say their daily prayers? : do they seem models of purity and restraint? : do they faithfully follow the holy precepts? : and the White Virgin acts as if she hasn't heard : she changes the subject : little Adelaida is playing the violin, she says : the latest waltz : young Master Jorge is looking through his telescopes : Don Agustín is reviewing his account books : because she's really looking at you, and if she tells the Master what you're really up to he'd unleash all the fires of hell : because although night has fallen and the bell's rung to signal quiet-time, she sees you scurrying over to the warehouses and shacking up with the negresses and letting them tempt your imps : little Fermina is reciting a beautiful poem by Alphonse de Lamartine!, says the Virgin : the one that starts pourquoi gémis-tu sans cesse, ô mon âme? : the Master Above fans himself under his mosquito net, swigging West Indian rum, but he's still thinking about you, the

Lequeitio niggers : have they cut the cane for grinding? : have they cleaned the press? : are they seeing to the bins and pans? : and this and that, not forgetting a thing : who's beating the pulp? : who's stoking the fires? : who's taking the trays to the sheds? : who's loading and laying out the bagasse? : and the White Virgin weeps silently and puts her hands over her face because it's pitch-black in Cruces and instead of sleeping and recouping your strength for the good of your souls and the profit from your bodies you surrender to all kinds of orgies and witches' sabbaths : and the good Father still goes on : tell me, daughter, are those blackies reciting the Pater Noster, Ave María, Credo, Articles of Faith and Works of Mercy? : do they know slavery is a gift from Heaven and that idleness breeds sin? : little Fermina's reciting J'ai cherché le Dieu que j'adore partout où l'instinct m'a conduit, says the White Virgin : Don Agustín's inspecting their weekly tallies : little Cecilia's embroidering beautifully! : the poor girl would like to help, to tell the Master of the Sugar-Mill in the Sky that, niggers though you may be, you strive sincerely to be good : but, what do you expect her to do? The Overseer's Son also keeps watch and notes down your errors in the Book : you can never melt away entirely into the black of night : the sweat, groaning and sour little smells you give off betray you : what biting, what heaving, what hugging, what squeezing, what heavy breathing! : wild beasts and animals of the forest show more self-control : at least they don't sin : they're total brutes, lack souls : you have one : puny, forlorn and sickly, but redeemable, nevertheless : and that's why you work from dawn to dusk : to save your souls : and rather than advancing and improving your stock you walk backwards like crabs : the Virgin would prefer to close her eyes and cover her ears, because the Master's left his hammock and is sharpening the edge of his Collins machete and if he peers over the terrace and sees you he'll descend like lightning and punish you : that's why she acts so absentmindedly and repeats Lamartine's verse and hums little Adelaida's waltz : because the things she sees in the storehouses would terrify the very devils in hell : it's not even normal copulation, the act of creation as contemplated by the canons : the propagation of the species is a noble end, even when they're dark obstreperous children : what's happening here, down below, cries out to Heaven for vengeance : you're wild beasts naturally depraved and always acting unnaturally! : you force your negresses to turn over and seek out their hind parts, drilling vile tunnels into their wicked blackness : and worse still : you order them to kneel before you and lift your burnt cane to their lips and stick it in : so they can savor its sweetness and squeeze out every last drop of treacle : and don't say it's not true because I've got my witnesses : your eyes bulging out of their sockets, you tremble, possessed and pleasuring like jungle animals! : and the females, My Lord, just look at them! : what shaking, what rubbing, what stroking, what laughter, what festing!

the chaplain seems about to choke : he turns red, perspires, grunts, foams at the mouth : the description of the nefast vices enacted in the storehouses brings flowery Latin phrases to his lips as he tries to place a flimsy veil of modesty, nay, a thin varnish of culture, over the crude frightful reality of those acts : cunnilingus, fellatio, osculos ad mammas, coitus inter femora, immissio in anum! : expressions that he forces out of his throat with obvious difficulty and which, to make it all crystal clear, he accompanies with epileptic gestures, frantically waving his arms, convulsing

you will divide the imaginary scene into two parts : or rather : into two opposing sets of words : on one side nouns, adjectives, verbs indicating whiteness, brightness and virtue : on the other, a lexicon of shadows, blackness and sin : the Master of the Sugar-Mill in the Sky swings in his hammock wearing a suit and a panama identical to your great-grandfather's, sharpening his splendid Collins machete and smoking a Havana cigar behind the gauze of his mosquito net : the White Virgin busies herself with the trifling but essential tasks in the Ancestral Home, conscious of an inner mastery she doesn't flaunt, wearing her chaste Sunday best over her pale blonde svelte shape : small winged mulatto putti playfully fend off the flies with large fans

Marita, daughter, can you hear me?

yes, Papa,

I don't know what's wrong with you today : it's as if you're in a haze

true : it must be the heat

I was asking after the Lequeitio estate : what's the time there?

according to my watch ten-thirty sharp

has the bell rung to get them inside and quiet?

yes, Papa

and where are the slaves?

where do you think they are? : in their huts

asleep by now?

I suppose so

I think you've got it wrong again: go on, take a look down there

the Mistress walks out to the mansion's colonial portico and fo-
cuses her opera glasses on the sugar-mill storehouses : though it's
the middle of the night they gleam and glint : brown faces, dark
hands, shadowy members, ebony bodies : all jet-black, mourning
and coal : the panting and copulating suggest wild beasts banquet-
ing in the darkest recesses of their recondite lair : making sure
Great-grandfather can't see her, she whispers to the chaplain
what are they doing?
he's floundering desperately like a fish out of water and puts his
hands to his neck to stop himself from choking : anger has given
way to sad despondency : he looks like an Ecce Homo
Lord, take this cup from me!
what cup?
no, I was only quoting
I can't see a thing : these glasses get blurrier and blurrier
just as well!
come on, tell me, I'm in a hurry
no, I can't
don't be such a turn off!
my lips hesitate to paint such a scene
hey, kid, don't get all fastidious on me
I don't dare
do it for Me
it's really ghastly!
well, give it to me in Latin
the chaplain crosses himself several times : the grim visions from
the storehouses have apparently driven him crazy : he struggles
violently with himself and finally his voice breaks out all atremble,
punctuated by bouts of shaking

membrum erectum in os feminae immissint!
socios concumbentes tangere et masturbationem
mutuam adsequi!
penis vehementis se erixet tum maxime cum crura
puerorum tetigent!
anus feminarum amant lambere!
sanguinis menstruationis devorant!
coitus a posterioris factitant!
ejaculatio praematura!
receptaculum seminis!

interruption, hollow silence : like when you stop writing : the Mistress will take a flask of smelling salts from her corsage and you'll make the chaplain inhale it avidly so he doesn't faint : the moans from the holding get hoarser and hoarser and, horrified, she'll try to cover her ears : Great-grandfather, in his hammock, begins to show signs of impatience
Marita!
coming!
the Mistress quickly fixes her face and squirts it with scent from her vaporizer before returning to the sitting room : she's always been kindly disposed towards the blacks and invents little white lies
the night is just divine! : it makes you feel like sitting in the arbor and gazing at the stars through young Master Jorge's telescope
why did you take so long? : did you bump into anyone?
the priest
and what did he have to say?
that the slaves are resting

do you know if they said their night-time prayers?

yes, I think so

and recited their acts of faith, hope and charity?

that too

and asked to be granted good deaths?

yes, as well as the Lord's Prayer for souls in purgatory and the prayer to the Holy Guardian Angel

very good! : long may they persevere! : why, I even feel like visiting the compound and blessing their slumber

no, you'll catch a cold!

didn't you say it was a marvelous night?

a cold wind came up

I'll bundle myself up

no, you stay there, I want to read you a poem

she runs anxiously to little Fermina's book cabinet and comes back with a quarto volume in a pretty leather binding

I'm really crazy about that Alphonse Lamartine : you know his "Le papillon"?

no

just wait and I'll read it

Marita, you know my French is terrible

never mind : I'll translate it afterward

the Mistress of the Sugar-Mill in the Sky recites slowly, in that sophisticated elegant tone little Fermina also adopts when declaiming

> naître avec le printemps, mourir avec les roses
> sur l'aile du zéphyr nager dans un ciel pur
> balancé sur le sein des fleurs à peine écloses
> s'enivrer de parfums, de lumière et d'azur

21

Great-grandfather listens fascinated and, thanks to her pious stratagem, yet again he'll forget those blackest of black sinners in Lequeitio : at a discreet signal from the Girl, the mulatto putto pours him
out his favorite punch, rum distilled in Massachusetts, water, sugar
and a few drops of lemon
your French sounds beautiful!
you're right : the fact is I find that Lamartine really inspiring, you
know? : he's what they call a terrific poet : besides, he's deeply
Christian : shall I read another, Papa?
as many as you'd like, Fermina, as many as you'd like

you'll continue uninterrupted, glancing at the attic ceiling and
the green-tiled sink, the engravings, the book with the drawing of
the vacuum evaporator, the photocopies of the Reverend Duke of
Estrada's catechism for blacks, soiling the hateful blankness of the
page with your one-franc-fifty ballpoint, giving the wretched pater
time to recover from his fright, shake the dust off his soutane and
biretta, clear his throat to speak, rehearse sweet smiles and extend
his arms paternally over the mill's recalcitrant holding

so, my children, why do you think you were brought here from the
remote jungles of Africa if not to be redeemed through toil and
shown the straight path to Christian salvation? : don't be distressed
by the grievous burdens you suffer : your body may be enslaved :
but your soul is free to fly to the happy resting place of the chosen :
that is why we sent our gunboats and brigs and made you cross the
briny : fettered and chained to stop the devil from tempting you

to return to your cannibal lives in the jungle, to the soul-sapping idleness of the basest of animals : defending you against yourselves : so one day you might sit at the right hand of the Father, enraptured by a thousand sublime and blissful visions : your souls as white as the purest sugar : the Master of the Sugar-Mill in the Sky will smile benevolently down and nobody will throw your black color, frizzy hair, squat noses, bestial lips in your face : your trials and tribulations will be over at last : the White Virgin will sit you at her table and fête you with her own delicious dishes : instead of wasting away in vile blackness, eternally tainted, you'll gradually enhance your spiritual stock, improve the terrible somber quality of your souls : the Master Above has taken pity on your condition and will rescue you from the gloomy shadows where you dwell and pursue lives of cleansing penitence : what an enticing comforting prospect! : slavery is the divine grace by virtue of which you will enter Heaven, immaculate and sparklingly white : the Son of God, like the overseer, keeps a watchful eye on your toil : an' like de overseer down 'ere 'e inspect the cuttin', loadin' an' haulin', an' never forget the old women an' mulatto kids gatherin' the cane dat dropped by the wayside, an' den go to the refinery an' inspect the Fawcett an' review the panner an' stoker slaves, an' those who shape the loaves, dry, select, an' package dem, so do dat Overseer in the Next Life keep a daily tally of your acts : He forget nothing, note everything down : He be like master sugar-maker too : just the same as Messié La Fayé, just the same : you seen him in his bowler and morning coat examining the vats in the purging room? : only he know the sugar's secrets, the kind of cane that work best, the right degree of concentrate, the amount of lime for the syrup : just as the Master Sugar-Maker in the Sky know every soul's nooks and crannies : who toil with a happy heart and who from fear of the lash, who accept hardship with resignation and who put up with it reluctantly : everything you do, say or think, he register straight away : he go daily to see the father an' show him the record sheet : Don Agustín, at the mill, keep a tally of the newly born, the sick, the dead, the escapees and the injured : the other Master also read the overseer's records and watch over the holding from Above : out in the plantation and in the refinery, in the press and the cauldrons, in the stores and the drying room, in the still and at the smithies : who leads the oxen, who cuts wood, who drags the cane, who takes the bagasse out : one day the world will end and it'll be like the young master's and misses' birthdays and saints' days : just like Don Agustín punishes and forgives on advice from the overseer, so God will condemn or save the souls of slaves according to their record cards and tallies : the light on one side and the dark on the other : some packed and shipped off to Heaven, others booted down to Hell or sent to the Purging Room : the docile slave's clean and his unblemished crystalline perfect soul is like white sugar, its grains sparkling, containing no dirt or slurry : but no soul starts out that way : they're all soiled by shavings or the greenish sugar that comes out of the bins : and to get them clean they have to endure a long, arduous process of purging : first cooked in pans like the syrup in the Jamaican train, going from one cauldron to another in order to be decanted, cleared and finally become sweet pulp : in each vat, the liquids bubble and evaporate, lose roughage and waste : you ever seen the yellow foam sediment the syrup gives off? : that's how the soul is purified and cleansed day after day and year after year thanks to the dear yoke imposed on you by your toil, and yet, my little children, when the pulp reaches the strike-pan, the consistency's still not right : it

24

must go to the cooling room and be beaten hard till it crystallizes : so too your soul : we must separate the pulp from the sugar, put it in trays to sit and purify : the stillness and pressure make the green impure slush run off : gradually the sugar on the top clears, but will-power and fine feelings alone aren't enough to do the job : doesn't a watery silt still have to be added, so the water can filter through the loaf and wash off the specks sticking to its crystals? : like the overseer handing out repulsive humiliating chores : thus the black in your soul runs off and you get brighter : and just as the purifying of sugar lasts thirty or forty days, the soul's cleansing can take thirty or forty years : but what does such a pitiful interlude matter compared to the immortal glory the Eternal One is offering you! : so don't curse your fate or become disheartened : all this affliction is needed in order to whiten your souls properly : one day they'll come out like sugar-loaves and be set to dry : the Overseer Up Above will come with his machete and cleave the loaf in a single stroke from the white layer at the base to the black on top : and it will be like Judgment Day : the black souls will be gone forever, like the burnt sugar that's thrown away : the cones and sacks, full of filth and impurities, that nobody would want to buy : the middle part of the loaf, the flawed sugar, which will have to be purged and cooked again till no trace of sin remains : and the transparent lumps at the base, the good and superior whites, the slaves who've diligently, zealously carried out all the overseer's tasks : the saved souls, the arctic steppes, the eternal glaciers of Nordic whiteness!

you will tackle the description of an Alpine landscape : Megève, Saint-Moritz, Andermatt? : Chamonix, Closters, Saas-Fee? : the Swiss Tourist Office offers you valuable help with a rich package of leaflets and brochures : log cabins, Christmas firs, the schizophrenic glare from snow-covered slopes : you review them one by one, seduced by the gleaming vistas, till your attention is caught by a color photograph illustrating the delights of Davos : agile deer-drawn sledges glide gently along the path and a spirited wind stirs up a delicate dancing flurry of flakes : the members of the distinguished family arrive suitably equipped for the weather and the occasion : ermine topcoats, resplendent fur hats, white mink-lined muffs and gloves : Great-grandfather Nicholas and the Czarina pose, stockstill, happy to encompass at a glance the immaculate symbol of their power, the dazzling mirage of a harvest of sugar : as well as Czarevitch George engrossed in the sight of wuthering heights through the lens of his telescope : the little grand-duchesses stroking the back of a stag, making snowmen or sitting astride a wise and knowing St. Bernard : all limpid and glinting, pure and beyond reproach : showing none of the vices and ailments that tropical climes spawn in so many fragile ivory bodies : stains, perspiration, heat, dust, insect bites : at the height of their radiant saccharine whiteness : generously exposed to the enraptured gaze of the holding staring with you at the slide show : while the chaplain continues to consult the pages of his catechism and goes on with his stubborn indoctrination of the black horde : as squat-nosed, alas, as they are dim-witted : spelling out the abysmal differences separating Great-grandfather from the Congo, the Czarevitch from the Calabar, the Davos ski slopes from the common trench in Lequeitio : pointing out the path of perfection but rubbing in the gravity of their criminal erring ways

you're to blame because you don' obey the rules : you're many, and there's only one overseer : today one of you go' missin', tomorrow another, one day another's up to no good, the next day another : every day overseer at end of his tether : one of you hide' on the track up to the hills, another squat' down while cuttin' cane, another neglect' the sugar loaves : a load of devious cunnin' pygmies : lookin' for a thousand ways to get out of workin' : and the overseer has to keep an eye on everyt'ing : on the mill, the pans, the still, the drying house : makin' sure t'is workin', copin' day and night with your tricks and slackin' : tom asleep next to the furnace, dick pausin' while pumpin' juices, harry shootin' the breeze behind the mill : day in day out : no Sunday day of rest for him : he has to check that you're cleanin' the sluices, scourin' the cauldrons, loadin' the bagasse, purgin' properly : Don Agustín only want statistics from him, and if he get angry, he'll chuck him out : and you're no help : that's why the Overseer Up Above go wild, and, when you're least expecting it, punishes you : and one day one of you get strung up and go straight to Hell or lose an arm in the Fawcett or cut his foot off with his machete or fall in the vats and is hauled out dead : and then who get bawled out by the master : you niggers? : nosiree : the overseer! : he tek rap for everyt'ing : machinery and tools, holdings, animals, food : he responsible for everyt'ing that moves in the mill : he handle' the breakdowns, upsets, difficulties, tribulations, problems : and to cap it all you complain : the shifts, the lash, the dogs, the lack of sleep : but take heed : the sparrows in the sky sleep less than you and never whine : why should you need more sleep? : look how cheerful they are, chirping gleefully when dawn breaks : God help the early riser and better a wakeful nigger than a snoring hick : lion get' no sleep and is king : the clock turn twenty-four hours and once wound never stop : first up get the best beans : an' you're still going on about lack of sleep! : the Master Up Above and the White Virgin never rest : are always lookin' down,

towards Cruces, mindful of that sugar-mill in Lequeitio : they don'
sleep five hours like you, or four or three or two or one : on duty
all week, on watch, on standby! : and they don't grumble about the
food : that there's only sweet potato and plantain and bits of bone,
a black mushy revolting mess : look at the farm animals : they don't
expect cod and jerky, tripe, rice, fine dishes : never throw away
their bowls if the grub's not to their liking : why should you behave
worse than them? : and still you want the overseer to turn a blind
eye and back off : as if he had endless reserves of patience, as if he
not already too easy on you! : bad bread, you say : wait, and it'll
turn good : hunger will make you think it's soft, nay, white wheat : no
one can have everything he wants : all we can do is to not want what
we can't have and cheerfully take what we're offered : a well-trained
belly embracing deprivation is freedom's great gift : how beautiful
it would be if rather than muttering and cursing your fate, you were
to meditate on Seneca's profound words to Lucilius in his letters : I
have tried to accustom myself to all that is adverse and onerous so
that I do not obey God but rather consent to everything he sends
me : I follow him as a matter of will, not from need : nothing that
happens makes me complain : what sublime thoughts out of a pagan mouth! : and, reborn now in your baptismal waters, your path
to salvation clearly drawn thanks to a providential heavenly plan,
you still refuse to accept your fate and only obey with the greatest
reluctance! : worse still : you're insolent : you strut and cheat and
defy the overseer, make threatening obscene gestures at him : then
moan if he claps you in the stocks and whips the skin off your
backs : overseer nasty an' 'andin' out bad punishment for next to
nuttin' : as if he hadn't already had it up to here with your sins and
wicked ways! : he's already been too soft! : then one day he snaps

and lashes out : and rather than repenting and seeking his forgiveness, the moment he lets you out, you start drawing your lines and circles on the walls of the storehouses : preparing your spells, getting your revenge, intent on trapping his spirit in the pot, willing misfortune, disease and destruction on him

to the ceiba, to the ceiba! : it's midnight, the witching hour and the slaves scurry stealthily out of their barrack-huts and cross the sleeping compound, egged on by the delirious chaotic geometry of the stars : the dogs lie poisoned by the water trough and the night watchmen snore in their sentry-boxes, deep slumbers brought on by powder the witch-doctors furtively dissolved in their daily ration of rum : a hot sensual tropical night out of an Elvira Ríos song, a night swooning on the sand, no, on the paths and shortcuts that, past the trays of bagasse, lead to the hills and mountains where the runaways are holed up : guiding them through a baroque profusion of lianas and ferns thanks to an esoteric alphabet, a secret unspoken code : rustling wind, buzzing insects and raucous birds weave a subtle web of complicity while the sugarocrat family trust credulously in their Guardian Angel's talismanic protection : no, that can't be right, the slaves must have knocked them out as well by cleverly spoiling their Brillat-Savarinesque gourmet platters : a plump chubby-cheeked angel, stuffed with heavenly creams and Capucin Gourmand delicatessen, apparently immersed in the speleological depths of the deepest of siestas : clearly not noticing the shadows slipping stealthily between the sheltering crests of the trees and the snaking curling foliage : to the clearing carved out by machetes and axes around the proud solitary ceiba tree : invoking the occult powers of the pot, already fed by four small piles of earth, hens' feet, beef, the master's own cigar butts : the witch-doctor recites his spells and litanies and, suddenly, the devil consents and Great-grandfather is caught : the small dishes contain hairs from the brushes and combs used by Great-grandmother and the girls and a toenail that belonged to young Master Jorge : one after another, all the members of the family meet the same fate : the drums beat in a frenzy and, summoned by powerful spells, they re-emerge, symbolically, on the podium in all their perfection and sovereign whiteness : the master, behind the wedding veil of his mosquito net, checking the account-books to the rhythm of his hammock's gentle to-and-fro : Great-grandmother, in the act of fulfilling her Marian devotions before serving dinner : young Master Jorge, with his globes and telescopes : the girls, at their embroidery, violin lessons and declamation of poetry by that Lamartine fellow who so bowled over the White Virgin : spotlights hidden in the branches of the ceiba draw brushstrokes of light over them and, keeping to the injunctions of cinematic precepts of old, you proceed rapidly to the selection of the elements to best fill your frame : like an expert French Film Institute graduate, searching out the ideal close-up, the significant illuminating detail : Great-grandfather's tense fingers sharpening his machete, a Czarina's ivory hand blessing their meal, little Jorge's Goyesque-Bourbon-ish gesture, chasing away flies, little Telesfora's pincushion bristling with needles, Fermina's flushed cheeks reciting Lamartine, Adelaida stiffly playing the romantic "Waltz of the Waves" on her violin : arm in arm, they come to the front of the stage to receive their applause and at that moment like a man furtively hatching an insidious plot the warlock witchdoctor prophesies catas-

30

trophe : sickness, ambushes, plague, misfortune, accident, war?
: worse, much worse! : streams of sweat will begin to ooze from
their brows, their temples, the diaphoresis gradually drenching
shirt-collars and the taffeta hems of dresses : dark greasy stains
will appear around the armpits of Great-grandfather's jacket and
the moisture from the Czarina's dipping neckline slowly saturates
her white satin breasts : impossible to hold back the sweat! : it's
futile to fan yourself, standing on the balcony, sipping sedatives,
wiping your face with a linen cloth : the glands in the mouth
in turn secrete a watery humor and the liquid leaks from the
corners of your lips and dribbles down your chin : drool, spittle,
saliva, phlegm, all running into nasal mucous and fluids, a single
yellow ductile mix that no handkerchief in the world could wipe
away : a tissue?, anyone got a tissue? the girls chorus : for though
still pre-pubescent, three red stains have simultaneously outraged
their immaculately white skirts in the place where the gazes of the
stolid sons of Sansueña like to linger : signaling to the shadowy
assembly that summer is here at last : and its bloody first fruits
wet and drench the cloth and spread the symptoms of those succulent hemorrhages : mysterious eruption of the nubile moment,
exalted in all climes and latitudes with elaborate sacrifices and
celebrations! : unable to endure the tortures of Tantalus, the best-
looking blacks rush onstage : embrace the trembling knees of the
maidens who are still maidens but girls no more, eagerly lifting up
their skirts and avidly applying thirsty lips to the
in Latin, in Latin, the White Virgin implores
but, although you try to oblige and write sanguinis menstruationis lambent, you find it impossible to continue : you don't have
the right Latin declinations and verbs : you're no Cicero, and your

poor jingoistic schooling taught you nothing : returning to your vernacular, to your common and garden variety, you proceed mosaic fount where lushes like to wet their lips and explore so expertly, so nimbly, the mounds' salients, nooks and crannies : right away, not holding their quills back for a second : while the once-upon-a-time girls look to the heavens like enraptured ecstatic Madonnas : or that saint in a trance in Alacoque getting her Big Promise : here is his Heart that hath so loved men, that hath spared naught to the point of collapse and self-destruction to show them his love! : his beatific angel face and eyes in thrall to a thousand glorious visions : demanding reparations from a contemptuous ungrateful world : and guaranteeing abundant, most special graces to his true devotees : also on bended knee, in delirious refreshing deliquescence : but the mill owners and Czarevitch gaze upon the scene with you and the deep hollow sockets of their eyes shine with horror : mon Dieu, quoi faire? : the power in the pots is mighty indeed and any attempt to resist is doomed to failure : squirming under their burden of shame, they swivel round on their heels, commendably turn their backs on you, only to reveal to the astonished assembly the humiliating color of their rear hemispheres : a non-sublimated, non-hidden, non-odorless, non-aseptic visceral explosion no strongbox, tabernacle or WC could keep secret : noisily proclaiming "le mot de Cambronne" : their irrefutable membership of the species : the sad crouching humanity of habitués of the trench : and, though forewarned by hoots of laughter, they see the disaster only when it's too late : their plebeian sludge unceasingly extends its radius of action, infects trousers, pollutes petticoats : in vain they grasp at hanging lianas and rehearse the magic gesture of pulling the chain : the divine trump won't flush ; the engineers must

be back in England : and to the delight of the holding they go on
ejecting dark ignominious matter until the moment the pots lose
their strength, the bright spotlights dim and, suddenly, on with the
motley : the slaves scatter in every direction : somebody's sounded
the alarm and the mill bell is tolling : the watchmen awake, they
and their dogs rush in at the overseer's urgent call : shouts, voices,
barking, lights, whistles : the ancestral hunt gathers : the august
family sleeps on : the chaplain will speak

and then you run away
reject succor from our light
repudiate whiteness
embrace the shadows of barbarism
elemental opacities
the somber splendors of their ceremonies attract you
warily
by night
you seek shelter and protection
in dark ravines and abysses
in the natural matrix of the caves
stealthy and cunning
night guides you
you put your trust in her
darting furtively like jungle beasts
vigorous and alert like savages
you elude our earnest desire to save you
from the brush and inclement weather
the dense forest absorbs you

hinders our plans for recapture
our gangs and armed posses
chase you in vain
along danger-infested tracks
you defend yourselves cruelly
with sly ruses and traps
sink stakes into paths
shoot sharp-pointed arrows
surprise us with your spears
hiding in burrows and crags
erect palisades and nets against the mares of the rancheadores
ambushes set in swamps and scrubland
you drop your rags to put our dogs off your scent
scale steep peeks
helped by ruthless runaways
and in your dens and hideouts
re-invent life in the wild, in the horrendous African jungle
deaf to our generous pardons give yourselves up to idolatry and vice
scorn the splendid benefits of slavery
eternal redemption through toil
the rest you know
the wrath of Heaven
divine punishment
righteous implacable revenge
so don't be upset if
when they find your secret retreats
our men treat you badly, cut off your ears and send them to the master
they are righteous men
and their punishments

bring joy to the hearts of the Great Overseer and bountiful White
   Virgin
that's why
your resistance
forces them to use their machetes and make you pay for your
   insolence
let no one be deceived and call them cruel
if they behead your leaders and post these trophies in streets,
   avenues and plazas
as examples to the unwary
a lesson to fools
crawling with filthy flies
mounted on the point of a spear

they are usually secured by placing the left leg of one
and the right of another in the same set of irons and by
hanging these on a cord they can walk very slowly : each
group of four is joined by the neck with a rope of twisted
strands : at night their hands are fettered and sometimes
bound together by a light chain : other slatees cut a piece
of wood about three feet long, drive a groove in the side
and slot in the malcontent's ankle enclosing it in a sturdy
iron ring
to ensure the boat's safety it is necessary to fetter and chain
them and shut them in the hold at night and even by day
when there's a storm : usually they get upset and sickness
and disease make them hate exercise so they're forced
to eat and dance under the lash so they look healthy when

they reach the market : it is also necessary to take precautions against attempted suicide

those who are up for sale are kept in a big corral : buyers inspect them carefully finger them make them jump kick the ground and stretch arms and legs : they force them to turn around and test them a thousand ways until they are sure they are fit and healthy

when informed that there is a male runaway hiding in the hills they pick up their shotguns and take along twenty men on foot : when he sees the crowd of people approaching he takes fright and grabs a stone to defend himself : he seeks refuge in the gully of a crag where they can't follow him : they gather firewood, pile it by the other entrance to the gully and set fire to it : it burns the boy's skin off forcing him to run out and jump into a pond : they order another nigger to pull him out but he resists ferociously : they pepper him with grapeshot and throw rocks at him : drag him along badly injured and force him to kneel : he gestures asking for water : they refuse and as soon as the hole is ready they put him in and cover him with earth even though he is still alive

the fugitive's head sits atop the stake like a strange knob on a walking stick and flies swarm over the gawping eyes nostrils swollen lips holes from the severed ears the clots of blood from the neck sliding down the gnarled surface of the pole

you break off your perusal of these documents : phrases culled from books and photocopies imprint themselves on your memories of the female slave's letter to your great-grandfather, resurrecting undiluted your hatred of the stock that gave you life : an original sin, its indelible stigma insistently harassing you despite your intrepid concerted efforts to set yourself free : the virgin page combines a delightful possibility for redemption with the pleasure of profaning its whiteness : a mere squiggle of the pen suffices : you'll try your luck again

selecting the sexy fat lady on the record from all the negresses : carefully permed hair, smooth bulging forehead, bushy eyebrows, broad flat nose, large gleaming white teeth, pink flickering tongue, dark tanned skin : two gold-plated earrings dangling, apparently jangling sweetly while she gleefully guarachas to the bilingual legend on the LP sleeve : humble demure house-proud now : performing her domestic duties accompanied by the purest of husbands : doubtless waiting for the Pigeon's surprise visit : in the meantime arranging her boy-to-be's diapers : the ever-blessèd fruit of her belly : namely you : in this dark humblest of hovels where her spouse plies his poor yet respectable trade : with the innate rather stylized elegance of those wholesome pilgrims from the Mayflower represented in the Massachusetts Wax Museum : both wearing simple, becoming tunics : austere sandals : captured at the very moment he wields chisel and plane and she sews so finely : the benign presence of domestic animals completes the peaceful tableau of honesty, happiness and hard work : the selection being particularly apposite : a likeable placid ox, a smiling sheep, a resurrected soft-fur jenny, a tame lambkin : your mother-to-be sings a simple cradlesong and the providential guardian of the house constructs a crèche for its auspicious animals : anything else? : of course : the holy Guardian Angel ever watchful, gliding protectively over the hovel on the whitest of extended wings : a few other elements are missing from the picture, so you add them in : two shining crowns, like rings of Saturn, encircle the holy couple's skulls, their glowing pates, in overt almost brutal defiance of the law of earthly gravity and a new celestial messenger, unschooled in the subtleties of a go-between, will instruct the sublime couple in the canny tricks behind divine plans : graphically explaining, via luminous similes, the mysteries of the Incarnation and the Trinity : ever notice what happens when you stand in front of a mirror? : you appear there, your image is reproduced upon it : and if you so love the sight of yourself and kiss yourself on the glass, the kiss you've given yourself will leave a dark circle : so, three things converge in a single mirror : your person, your image and the dark circle made by your kiss : you created the image and in turn the dark circle comes from your person as well as the image the mirror reflects : thus, like a sunbeam, traversing sky-blue stained glass, and which turns as blue as the glass it has passed through, in no way defiling or tarnishing this color, so little Alvaro descending into this world to redeem the sins of the pariahs of this earth will pass through his Mother's body, partake of her flesh and blood, without rupturing or diminishing her immaculately virginal purity : the bright-winged catechist fades at a subtle tremor from your quill and your mother resumes her diligent labor and her blessed male continues chiseling the much vaunted crib : the message has illuminated the natural darkness of their minds and both ponder for hours on end the profound and wonderful mysteries revealed by the angel's words : she weaves and weaves while her husband sets up the crib and makes the preparations a host must make to welcome the Pigeon : arranging lovely welcoming nests

with a few fowl feathers : setting out miniature swings, small bowls
of bird food, clean and capacious drinking fountains : not sparing
a detail to make it feel comfortable and at home : above all, a soft
smooth eiderdown where the visited mother, when the time comes,
can brood on her illustrious, much coveted egg : and peer out the
window and watch the sky, trying to spot her swift and nimble visitor among birds swooping down over the mill : the other negresses
are also spying, hidden behind shutters and blinds, skeptical about
the heralded coming, envious of her unique privilege
wat do dat nigger t'ink actin' der queen wid dat flab lip she got an'
dat frizzy 'air an' a dingy-dark no God can creem dat we be below
'er an' dat she be goin' even bette' shakin' it wid a white sonovabitch
dat by me mudder be no gud fe coaly-coaly fer I do swear dat walk
by 'er in der night an' ya not got no candle lit ya no see 'er face!
but she acts deaf and scorns this scurrilous gossip, peering avidly at
the sky : at that very moment the prospecting columbide gently de-
scends over the hovel and flies around the expectant mother with
a thousand tender loving coos : then sways on the swing, settles on
the ox's neck, picks at the meal in the bowls, visits a water fountain : alternates graceful flight with a quick release of innocent pellets that the ever-so-cleanly servile patriarch rushes to remove : its
wings beat weightlessly near the anxious maternal mouth fanning
out protectively till they artfully veil her visage : the adept Pigeon
performs a singular acrobatic hoppity genesis, caroling ineffably
while the humble artisan weeps tears of joy and celebrates in ecstasy the sublime mystery of your Incarnation! : time and again
drying his eyes and weeping anew : thereby not noticing the appearance, visible through the gap in the window, of the imperious
figure of Changó

Changó?

Changó, that's right, grandson of Agayú and son of Yemayá and Orugán, lord of thunder and lightning : revered by the kneeling electrified holding as he crosses the mill-yard heading towards the hovel, invested with the special powers and gifts attributed him by the voodoo books heaped under your table : Santa Bárbara, too : though male, so very male beneath her skirts : looking for a fight, bold brave and fire-eating : with his bloodstained standard, swift-footed Arab steed and flaming sword : fierce lips projecting a false smile and a dazzling leonine moustache against a dark tanned face : refulgent flickering solar : tips twisting like whiplashes or lizard tails glinting rapacious eyes aimed in turn at the busy family and their Épinalesque domestic tableau : at the mother caught in the Pigeon's spell and the diligent lachrymose patriarch gathering up the visitor's exquisite droppings in the finest cloth : your huge undeniable presence now fills the spacious doorjamb and the meek animals in the picture look you up and down, show clear signs of distress : stirring uneasily beside the Christmas crib, fascinated by the beast leaping between your legs, and drawn to Yemayá's sweet decoy : but apparently the mystery's protagonists notice nothing and the bewildered Pigeon flies from the swing to your mother, from the food-bowls to the fountain, visibly enthralled by his own steaming pile of pellets : however its hour has come and a quick swipe from you is enough to annihilate it, reducing it to the tiniest heap of feathers : your steely incisors crush its fragile bones, innocent blood runs from your lips and enhances your moustache's sumptuous splendor : as the hapless body nourishes your well-protected prey, you send the boy with the towels away and close in on Yemayá : neither revealing revulsion at incest nor fleeing the palm tree's crest : gazing calmly at her sweaty brow, flickering eyelids and eager lips : still stunned by the deceased Pigeon's fleeting virtuosity on the wing but now ready to welcome the beast's imminent attack : the surly lethal creature you proudly display, waiting expectantly in your groin : in her ancient wisdom she volte-faces and offers her juicy posterior : the fiend can't wait to leap in and, though strait is the gate, you push hard, blood on fire, set on victory : forbidden possession of the mother performed in the most peculiar of postures : prints from an illustrated edition of the *Kama Sutra* inspire you with their musical variations on a theme : soloists and virtuosi, flautists, double-bassists, trios seemingly visit the whole range, rehearse the adagios, graves, ma non troppos, andantes, of a portentous maestro : with the nirvana-ish eternally vacant expressions on the faces of workers riveted to the vertiginous rhythms of a Taylorized factory in Detroit : assuming the most complicated positions, determined to emulate past gymnastic feats : the god's miraculous resources guarantee you victory, and, holding her aloft thanks to a subtle combination of knees and elbows, you extend your bold incursions while the other you awaits inside the imminent creation of its body : as yet immaterial, but already anticipating the closeness of its being and future, of a luminous destiny : the somber violent beast has settled in and you glory in its onslaughts : its spirited bellicose charges : watching it wallow, bite and cruelly bare its claws as the spellbound mother continues her esoteric twosome with her almost fully digested visitor, deceived no doubt by the light flurry of feathers that, on the outside, you now teasingly wave : faking caresses, billing and cooing, your fingernail imitating the scrape of its beak and your lips the faint beating of wings my love, my soul, my king, my Pigeon, is it You? : you say. yes,

41

my black beauty, yes, it's me, your lickle Pigeon, the best of the Trio, the Pigeon-Fanciers Federation's holy patron : and the rapturous ecstasies of the woman thus visited slowly ascend in tone to Himalayan paroxysms : her elemental warble, like the song of the hoopoe, gradually turns into the cry mezzo scream mezzo bleat, favored by feathered Tyrolean ramblers yodeling to one another across their country's mountains and climaxes in the stentorian bellow that, legend has it, Sir Edmund Hillary and his faithful Sherpa Tenzing let out the second they stepped onto the roof of the world, up among the eternally snowy peaks : and thus embedded in the blackness of the nefast sibyl, existentially impatient, you watch out for the slow expansive spasms that will miraculously beget your body : thanks to your sage prescience in releasing the beast and allowing it to graze in that shady grove the Christian flock is authorized to visit on feast days in order to guarantee an orderly propagation of the species : you compel it to stretch out for a few seconds in that dreary abode and to empty the sadness and woe out of its soul : but the gene cuts its path, sailing against the current, and will reach its appointed destination with mathematical precision : the maternal ovum, thus fertilized, that will finally give you being and constitute the starting point of your whole risky enterprise : nine months to go! : time to ripen and grow in the soft sphere of the egg : still unaware of your exact color, desperate to discover it in the mirror : the hopeful mother also waits, devoting body and soul to sewing the Boy's diapers : jealous, the other negresses are still muttering, because the news of your coming has spread and adepts bring their humble presents from all corners : a punnet of fruit, a bowl of Maggi soup, a tin of condensed milk, half a dozen eggs : and your mother smiles gratefully and continues

her sewing uninterrupted : the signs of the visitation start to become more evident : the dress in the picture gets tighter and tighter and she decides to make another that's neither shamefaced nor in your face : avoiding both the loose puritan prurience and blatant pride of your females, their bloated conceit in apparent defiance of public opinion : embracing neither extreme thanks to some old but nevertheless handy patterns from *Elle* and *Le Jardin des Modes* that are a model of grace, modesty and thrift : you busily go about your maternal tasks not realizing that your devotees are gearing up to surprise you with one fabulous present : the credit-card purchase in installments, of the latest model of Singer complete with guarantee : it's all sorted! : the heralded epiphany is nigh and the niggers gather in the mill-yard waiting on events in the hovel : the horoscopes of the best astrologers agree unanimously on the timing and you'll have to concentrate hard not to miss your exit : tense as a tightrope walker mid-air or a tumbler attempting a lethal triple jump : you leap out! : and don't need to open your eyes or rush to look at yourself in the mirror : you'll be fucked! : pale face as ever, a young Master, a shitty white : choruses of jeers from the indignant holding : cut off forever from pariahs and immigrants : no Only Child no Messiah no Redeemer
you?
      don't make me laugh!
             with that defect of yours?

II

1

when the strident voices from the country you despise offend your ears, you are astounded : what more do they want? : haven't you settled your account with them? : exile has turned you into a different being who has nothing in common with the one they knew : their law is no longer your law : their justice is no longer your justice : nobody is waiting for you in Ithaca : as anonymous as any foreigner, you will visit your own mansion and the dogs will bark at you : your scarecrow djellaba is taken for a common beggar's rags and you cheerfully accept their small change : disgust, commiseration, contempt will guarantee your victory : you are king of your own world and your sovereignty extends to every edge of the desert : clad in the rags of your original fauna, feeding on their leftovers, you camp on their garbage heaps and dunghills as you carefully sharpen the knife you will one day use to mete out justice : the freedom of the pariahs is yours, and you will not be turning back eagerly you grasp your magnificent anomaly

2

from all the beggars in the souk, you choose the most abject : the African harka demands total unreserved surrender and you've decided to take your promethean devastating passion to its ultimate delirious consequences : beauty, youth and harmony are dispensable accessories that likewise adorn the love that does dare speak its name and you inexorably cast them off to embrace the most vile alarming attributes of an illegal brotherly body : old age, filth and wretchedness sweep you up in an impetuous current, its pull irresistible and vertiginous : urine, grime, sores, suppurations are the daily bread you consume with solitary pride : Ebeh may not yet be in his thirties, but the plagues and diseases that come with extreme poverty have marked him with indelible signs of decrepitude : his shaven skull's an open sore, purulent scabs and boils show themselves between tufts of a grayish unshaven beard : hereditary syphilis has prematurely deprived him of his sight and the cartilage and cilia in his nose, and his ragged clothes barely hide the ancient scars and wounds extending from his neck to his instep : when you get close, he'll finger every inch of your face with his rapacious claws before broadening his toothless gawp into a smile and eagerly gripping your chest like an imperious falcon : shifting sands foreshorten the stormy traces of your caresses and your mutual imploring embrace gradually assumes the undulations of the desert : birds of prey tearing each other's flesh, in combat, in a sudden frenzy of caressing wings! : steel of curved beaks and sharpened spurs sinking into throbbing entrails, to the crowd's circus cries : likewise thirsting for blood as the battle reaches a paroxysm that brings a rough and rigorous remedy to passion's fury : thus provoking the combined disgust and pity of a noisy group of tourists prudently watching the spectacle from the boxes and stalls : French straight out of the pages of *Madame Express*, white middle-class gringo families, garrulous gesticulat-

ing Italians, some stolid sons of Sansueña : all fresh off a jumbo
jet with their usual photographic-cinematic gadgetry and attire
common to the planet of the apes, as in Ben Jelloun's spellbinding
poem : all warned in advance against the snares and dangers of
this suspect country and the proverbial duplicity of its dark cunning inhabitants
attention aux BICOTS
ils sont voleurs et puants
ils peuvent vous arracher votre cervelle
la calciner et vous l'offrir sur tablettes de terre muette
your voracious embraces earn reproachful looks, a perfect illustration in their eyes of the abysses of derision, filth and sin where the
terrible stock of the Agarene stews : they're horrified, but charita-
bly stoop over you with their cameras and, once they've snapped
the barbarous coupling for a future mondo cane museum of their
souvenirs, they try to palliate your baseness and sores with a mag-
nanimous shower of coins
oh, comme c'est dégoûtant!
take a look
I can't, it's so awful
ils s'enfilent entre eux en public!
tíos guarros!
si a meno fossero giovani
l'Arabo è vecchio e spaventoso
tu crois qu'ils comprennent le français?
essaye de leur parler
monsieur, vous n'avez pas honte?
execute them, sí señor, execute them
ah, just like the good old days!
it turns my stomach

io credevo che soltanto i ragazzi
quick, snap it!
please, don't move
try again
gentuza, eso es lo que son!
excusez-moi, monsieur, je suis sociologue et je mène une enquête sur
disgraziati!
honey, we're so happy together
guarda, carina, che porcaccione!
qu'est-ce que vous pensez du mariage? n'avez-vous pas nostalgie
d'une famille?
el matrimonio, sí señor!
la pareja, el hogar, los niños
à quel âge vous vous êtes rendu compte que
I'm getting sick
una fotografía ancora
une thèse sur les déviations pychologiques et sexuelles de
te das cuenta de nuestra suerte de haber nacido normales?
cuando pienso que habría podido ser como ellos
calla, chato, que se me pone la carne de gallina
avez-vous reçu une education quelconque?
oh!
what's up?
regarde, ils jouissent!
un momentino, per carità
look at this
andiamo, è troppo orrido
nos van a estropear la luna de miel
no te preocupes, cielo, ahora mismo vamos al cuarto y fabricare-
mos un nene

sí, hazme un niño rubito!

as the babelian crew scatters, one last bystander couple snaps a color close-up of the double body in crime : they're both young, beautiful and perfectly matched and they exchange happy knowing smiles crowned by the sovereign perfection of their teeth

3

in the center of the wedding bed and on the gleaming counterpane, your gaze lingers on your implacable enemy
the smiley
springtime
fertile Reproductive Little Couple
irrespective of ideologies or credos, all nations feed the myth, churches and governments unanimously extol it, various news media use it in their advertising campaigns : its image fills big cinema screens, is rehearsed obsessively, infinitely, on the pages of the dailies, puts in appearances along highways and subway tunnels, multiplying deliriously in the great picture tube's cyclopean eye : unblemished whiteness and scented tooth-pasty breath underline its natural harmony, facial cream and electric razors contribute to its well-being, menthol cigarettes stimulate and intoxicate it, domestic electrical goods reinforce its solid bonds, incredible instant detergents ensure its radiant future : airlines and tourist agencies frame it in a vast suggestive welter of landscapes, monuments and beaches : its tiny supine presence embellishes the tempting vista of an island paradise : blue transparent sea, languid airy coconut palms, soft fine sand, Polynesian cabins shaped like Vietnamese hats, na-

tive boatmen decorated with Gauguinesque flower garlands : the sophisticated drink of the month deliciously refreshes its jaws, a soothing suncream softens its golden skin, andrékostelanitz transistor music cradles its dreams of bliss, its symmetrically positioned bodies encouraging mutual ecstasy behind the double protection of dark diaphanous glasses : snapped in front of a bevy of noble ruins, blatantly exhibiting its panoply of pierrecardinesque clubmed accessories, it offers an image of cloudless happiness, within the means of any pocket : unisex shirts and jerseys, trousers in the most striking color combinations, time-keeping support from the Swiss watch industry, the latest miracle camera from the fertile Nipponese imagination : in the far distance, third-world natives wander on camels or donkeys and disappear amid palm or olive trees, behind brown hills or honeyed dunes : because everything, that's right, everything enhances its unique splendor, are subtle brushstrokes enhancing its exemplary beauty : lipstick, tissues, deodorants : Coca-Cola, ice-cold beer, scotch on the rocks : refrigerators, tape recorders, cars : holidays, psychiatrists, credit cards : gym, diets, anti-stress massages : and instead of aging and fading, falling ill or dying in an accident, it flourishes and rejuvenates, ever perfecting itself, admiring itself, seeking the means to self-perpetuate according to the canons of the sacramental rite : the range of models is vast and guarantees a splendid sumptuous ceremony : the bride is delightful in her white chiffon dress and tulle dream of a veil held in place by a simple though original headpiece : accompanied by her father, she reaches church in a handsome carriage pulled by two fine steeds and, once the emotion-charged ceremony is over, she and her fine figure of a husband move on to that renowned restaurant where an award-winning chef has laid out an

exquisite succulent banquet : and in front of the window displays at
El Corte Inglés, la Samaritaine, Macy's, or Bloomingdale's, the
dense motley crowd thronging the asphaltjungled sidewalks in the
hustle and bustle of rush hour stands and enviously inspects the
luxurious king-size bed destined to underpin a lengthy domestic
life of love, prosperity and happiness : an extra-firm lace-tied mat-
tress that assures proper support and lasting comfort : cash or easy
installments : complete with matching balanced foundation box
spring : do it now! : its design makes for easy sleeping : turn your
dreams into reality! : this week only at a terrific discount : make up
your mind, caramba! : this quilted, extra-firm favorite is for you! :
passers-by jostle on the other side of the window and elbowing
your way through, nose pressed against the plate glass, you too ex-
amine the other items in this fantastic bedroom : a luxurious three-
piece leather suite, two bedside tables with corresponding lamps, a
six-pronged Venetian chandelier, a beautiful dressing table, a con-
sole adorned with a huge bouquet of white lilies and spikenard : a
virginal Murillo print adds an elegant touch to the ensemble, complete with parallel image of the Redeemer pursuing whoever
looks his way with a silent desolate gaze, both pictures surveying
the scene from above the wedding bed : the Little Couple has just
arrived : in top hat and tails, the bridegroom carries his betrothed
in his arms and her blushes, though dimmed by the gauze of her
veil, gently pink her cheeks : he solemnly places her in the middle
of the eiderdown where the hallowed procreation is about to be
performed ad majorem Dei gloriam : the protagonists' sighs underline the supreme transcendence of their act and, out of an innocent sense of shame, as they begin to undress, they turn their
backs on each other : drape their symbolic beautifying garments

50

over his or her armchair, his or her side of the regal bed : the emotion coursing through the pair is evident and, despite the distancing Brechtian plate glass of the shop window, they win over the public that surrounds and bellows at you : all the prophets have sung to the miracle of genesis, so what about you, you wretch? : nonproductive loves, nefast pleasures, lewd couplings, and the rest! : time you revamped, time you plucked your lyre in tune! : the language's most luminous adjectives will flock to your pen and turn you into a novel Nobelizable bard to patermaternity! : your readers will breathe a sigh of relief, the critics will applaud and teaching manuals will proudly present your stirring human sentiments to be admired and worshipped by future generations! : the aura of historical responsibility weighs you down and you look around for guidance and inspiration : diverse poetry anthologies obligingly offer you their muse and you open one at random : how beautiful to live under one roof, both united forever in love blissful! : you always in love, I always satisfied, we two a single soul and a single heart, and betwixt us both, my mother like the Godhead! : reading these lines enthuses you wildly and a reedy voice encourages you to continue : go on, boy, carry on rhyming, see how easy it is : but the Little Couple has stripped naked and the wondrous events on the nuptial couch demand your full attention : sitting on a corner of the bed, jointly protected by Madonna and Redeemer, the spouses read aloud a selection of encyclicals on the marriage sacrament and its goals before consulting the latest illustrated edition of the *Manual for a Healthy Sexual Life* that the latest blessing from the Great Magus has authorized for today's newlyweds : to ensure a harmonious accord that, while bearing in mind the aim of procreation, allows the future parents a gentle, ever-so-restrained satisfaction : the color images provide a vast range of positions that favor sure-fire fertilization and the Little Couple study them while indulging in a little acceptable cuddling : pleasuring, shaking, flushed : already anticipating the tiny gentle penetration that will send the gene down the usual old path and fulfill, in months to come, its atavistic longings : positions number three, sixteen, and twenty-four seem to fall relatively within their scope and they decide to put them methodically and precisely into practice : crouching, facing each other, they perform various gymnastic-respiratory exercises with the aim of relieving nervous tension and facilitating a beneficial relaxation of the tissues : the manual's panoply of examples should allow the Couple to conjugate the verb to love in exemplary fashion, and the crowd of onlookers impatiently eye the spot where the bridegroom's shadowy thighs converge, waiting for irrefutable signs of his state of arousal : at first glance nonexistent, perhaps by virtue of the powerful self-control characteristic of men who exercise the iron discipline over their bodies that comes from mastery of yoga : serene, seemingly self-confident, he continues his inspiratory-expiatory movements for an hour that flex the muscles and flow of blood at the optimal critical moment : but despite his growing signs of fatigue and his bride's growing agitation, the tumescent flow is a no-show : no auspicious extension outstanding on the cusp of his groin and the bridegroom's boyish face gradually reflects a mixture of despair and embarrassment : manual, encyclicals, gym and yoga are not enough : he tries new breathing exercises in vain, stares at the book's color pictures, nit-picks Vatican Council doctrine with a fine-tooth comb : the prospects from his thighs remain ignominiously minimal and, as the present indicative goes quiet and hopes in the future recede, their amorous con-

jugating shifts to melancholy conditionals before slipping sadly
into the imperfect subjunctive :

if I had	you would have
if you had	I would have
if we had	we would perhaps have
if we had	we would never have

passive voice and perfect tenses don't fit the nuptial paradigm and,
in the absence of a nihil obstat, you must discard them : the Little
Couple's tribulations get increasingly pitiful and they futilely repeat gerunds and imperatives : the verb is irregular, if not defective
and is a non-event : and while the incurable participle whimpers
in sympathy, the confusion and dismay on their faces impacts the
sidewalk audience and gradually infects the huge mass of the city :
the exorcisms from your poetic compilation have no effect and you
hurl it angrily down the nearest sewer : for a few moments you feel
totally lost and meander, head bowed, among Manhattan's unruly
fauna : but destiny hasn't forsaken you and, when you raise your
eyes to heaven while waiting at a traffic light, you are blessed to
witness a sudden transfiguring Apparition

4

modern information theory and spectacular advances in cyber-
netics help us plot its preferences : countries with archaic, tribal,
predominantly agrarian-pastoral economies : mesetas and barren steppes parched by fiery droughts, swept by wintry northern

winds : semi-barbaric shepherd communities with high birthrates and almost nil schooling : it enjoys crags and gullies that allow it to display its gravity-defying gifts as a gymnast : from solitary tree, dainty meadow and crystalline spring fomenting popular beliefs to antiphonic chants : from damp secluded caves forged by the geological action of water underground, the ideal backdrop to its levitation and flights of fancy : it likes to hew a path through the clouds and float between gauzy veils and cottony tufts, competing with a dead envious sun that's forced to slink off and adorn its ears with the brightest stars : it doesn't scorn surprise appearances, particularly in front of children : it chooses them before they can read or know anything about radar or the pill : it is generous with its kind deeds and smiles, promises help and largesse, heralds revolutions and earthquakes and invents whimsical desires : its crown and mantle rival those of the best doll princesses and, when it speaks, it uses that country's voice, in shrill bright tones : a modern version, so cinema buffs say, of the unforgettable Shirley Temple

5

but you're a child no longer, no illiterate, no shepherd, and the miraculous apparition summoning you from the javelin of the Empire State Building is the wondrous King Kong : just freed from his chains in the burlesque Broadway exhibition, he's climbed to the skyscraper's pointed pinnacle and is now playfully pawing helicopters as they fly to Pan Am's roof : those unsuspecting machines hadn't rumbled that his presence wasn't a novel publicity stunt mounted by a tourist industry facing difficult times with the dollar in crisis, but shockingly splendidly for real : stripped of their passenger loads, they crash like dragonflies on the ant-like sidewalk bustle and your guardian faun gleefully applauds the panic and confusion : rapt maidens tremble in unmentionable bliss on his huge hairy palm, and the ecstatic anthropomorph gazes at them and brushes the tip of his darting tongue against their thighs : searching out the delicious periodic honey like those sweet-toothed bear cubs, bee-honey connoisseurs, who stick their snouts into hives completely oblivious to the insects' anger or tormenting stings : while they sigh, moan and melt joyfully on contact with his moist all-conquering fire : dreamily, they inspect the fantastic dimensions of his appendages and mouth the maxim wrongly attributed to St. Augustine : that most beautiful credo quia absurdum against which St. Buenaventura rebelled so petty-mindedly : unable to decide to reject the vertiginous crazy idea, like the oddball in the story : engrossed, like him, in contemplation that lasts hours and hours before sadly renouncing such madness : but the heroic feat tempts them, and the maidens curse and scream at the narrowness of the absurd fate that denies them access to this higher form of knowledge : the biblically immediate and total variety : no way, no way : all the Vaseline in the world wouldn't stretch to such a miracle! : the wretched newlyweds, now spent, witness his awesome display and shame anger and envy gradually darken their faces : his inferiority in respect of your mentor is conclusive and irremediable and the maidens notice it too and, suddenly all haughty, launch into futile humiliating comparisons : unlike the film's mega-well-adjusted heroine, able to pass without anger or sorrow from the arms of her illustrious abductor to those of her pathetically miniscule fiancé, the panoramic revelation from the pinnacle traumatizes the girls

55

to the end of their days, destroying any possibility of a hypothetical return to normal : gnosis was too powerful : henceforth, they will detest that tatty string of concepts and boring sequence of syllogisms : King Kong's solid materialism will pursue them wherever they go, together with the shining proof of his irrefutable arguments : and a honeymoon in Paris, as advised by the best doctors, only aggravates their fragile state of mind : the Eiffel Tower and Obelisk keep the poignant vision in the frame and rather than forgetting and putting it behind them, full of contempt and loathing they will discard the insipid miserable pleasures offered by the scholastics of matrimony : beneath the Arc de Triomphe, they dream of a necessary entrance into praxis : of the sudden brutal eruption of German philosophy, so similar to the one recently embodied by the Siegfriedian monster and his superior artillery, which gave that monument its raison d'être during the virile debacle of 1940 : identifying there and then with the emblematic symbol of their total surrender to the victorious orangutan : etched forever on their retinas in the fullness of his almighty power : eternally prepared for that qualitative dialectic leap : with King Kong, your master, aiming the clean lines of his wondrous categorical imperative at the center of their female selfness

6

you will follow their example and extol the simian's amorous weaponry : put your pen in the service of his magnificent excess, exalting his gifts with all the resources of your verbal insidiousness : through subtle venomous subversion of hallowed linguistic principles : sacrificing the referent to the truth of discourse, bowing to the after-effects of your delirious deviation : splendid loneliness of a long-distance runner : insolent defiance of the proper order : you will allow the Little Couple to reproduce while yawning politely and conceive and give birth to a disgusting babe : the flaccid inept offspring out of that saccharine song : a tiny tot? lots of boyish curls? : radio-requested lyrics make no difference : his various analnasalmouthy orifices excrete stinking secretions that gradually pollute the atmosphere in the ideal family home and precipitate sonorous visitations by ambulances and firemen armed with sanitizing tools and gas masks : tepid productive love is an immediate and total turn off and you will extol the solitary sterile pleasure, the shocking nefast illegal sort : inspired by King Kong's grandiose majesty you now sing of the abominable, the aberrant and the illicit : bring into the bright light of day the monsters that terrorize puny minds during the sleep of reason : abject copulations, seminal waste thrown up by bodies conjugated randomly in sumptuous exciting mutual festivities! : dreaming of a twilight maelstrom in an extinct universe, where the harsh raw love the simian arouses fosters all manner of crimes sheltered and stimulated by his savage might

7

in the present subsoil of Manhattan, down the labyrinthine network of tunnels and drains underpinning the island's profile, a community, no less complex and interesting than the one logged by sociologists, has established itself, lives and likes to spread through the

deep shadows of its Stygian lagoon : increasing numbers of croc-
odiles, caimans, lizards and iguanas infest the nauseating sewers
and, adapting to their unusual habitat, are slowly metamorphosing
to better suit their somber nocturnal existence : new amphibian
and frighteningly rapacious species multiplying stealthily without
raising the least alarm, under the feet of the ignorant ingenuous
city : crawling, slippery and shiny, they feed on its stinking waste
and await the opportunity to abandon their parasitic lives and take
an avenging look at the light of day : lowering yourself down rusty
little ladders, rushing through a maze of oozing passages, you contemplate the spasms of their gelid copulations and the oviparous
exits of their offspring : like the cyclopean eye, your inspiration always sparkles at night and the desire to be like them stirs insatiably
in the most hidden recesses of your soul : long sinuous body covered in the toughest of scales, large mouth and sharp teeth, webbed
hind legs and flat tail for swimming : abdicating from your illusory
role as king and master of Creation (vertical stride, articulated language, sensitive intelligent soul) to embrace the relentless rigor of
these accursed fauna : darkness and filth will be your hideout too
and out of the mouths of the sewers and the whole city's system of
supply and drainage, you and your brethren will infiltrate the tops
of skyscrapers and mount invasions of houses and apartments via
the drain-pipes from sinks, lavatories and bathtubs : sly sinuous
heads will spring from the bowl the instant a hominid starts to
lower his shamefaced posterior, and he will step back in horror, like
an unwary rambler turning a stone over with his stick and discovering a nest of vipers : but these reptiles are your friends and that
intimate familiarity brings you pleasures incomparably superior to
those offered from the eternal (artistic, moral, or social) casuistry

of the two-footed species : descent down the animal ladder is ascent for you : you bear the mark of Cain on your brow, and though
a heretic among heretics, you won't join the prayers and communions of their ardent liturgy, out of respect for the turbaned el-
ders who display their persuasive arts in Moroccan tourist leaflets
nonetheless your words will extol the clandestine guild of snake
charmers roaming in the night

8

when darkness brings to a close the reasonably productive activities of the busy city, the creature's adepts emerge from their usual
daytime lethargy and, after cautiously surveying the abandoned
sidewalks, wander furtively through dark deserted areas, completely ignoring the twilight propaganda posted by the ophidians'
adversaries
WATCH OUT : THEY ARE HIGHLY DANGEROUS
THEY ATTACK THEIR PREY BY INJECTING POISON
THEIR BITE IS ALWAYS SERIOUS AND OFTEN LETHAL
THEY SOMETIMES STRANGLE THEIR VICTIMS BETWEEN
THEIR COILS
THEY CAN BE MORE THAN FORTY FEET LONG
the envious arguments of these paterfamiliases don't deflate their
good spirits, and zigzagging around scary street-corners to put
possible persecutors off their trail, they explore the dark damp
places where the hated much feared animal likes to slink : mossy
flaking caves where the water's subterranean action creates drips,
waterfalls and stalactites dimly lit by a flickering bulb, the kind that

usually light cells and dungeons in the basements of police stations : secure, in an almost complicit penumbra, they wait patiently until he bursts in suddenly, enigmatically, then they kneel and pay him the customary courteous homage : savoring the advent of his sturdy virtue with the solemn gestures of those who shut their eyes in ecstasy when the magician places the pristine tablet on their tongues : kneeling on a modest rough-and-ready hassock, if not the ground : immersed in the epiphany of their sublime though non-communicable experience : not forgetting, afterwards, the customary giving of thanks : the acts of desire, abnegation and humility advised in the induction manuals : but the frenzied night goads them on, and abandoning the quiet solitude of the crypt, they proceed tirelessly and diligently on their haphazard schedule of visits : through gloomy waterlogged zones that favor their secret sucking activity : not to forget the dense natural terrain of parks where the cruel cunning animal intuitively hides : guided by a mysterious sixth sense along trails and shortcuts until they discover the green hedge that acts as a nest and hides their abject genuflections from the world's gaze : orders, threats, exorcisms don't succeed in putting them off their hunt and in thrall to their wild devotions they scorn impending dangers with a recklessness they relish : they continue beating despite the foul weather, the rules and regulations of the close season and hysterically wailing patrol cars : inquisitorial torches illuminate the night above their heads and their loud echoing footsteps further heighten the risks posed by their sacramental liturgy : a successful resolution of the ceremonial exorcism finally brings them onto low swampy ground, and, unseen, you sneak quietly in their wake across filthy trailing vegetation : through strata upon strata, where myriad wandering shadows pace in ghostly robes, in the haze from small anemic lamps and rising steam : from purifying subterranean pools to the shadowy cages that usually shelter the rampant beast's robust bulk : the tenacious crafty ophidian, whose hiss the alert ear of the hunter strains to detect : yes, it's there, and everything seems to indicate that it's waiting to paralyze the unwary visitor with venom from its voracious mouth, or else via subtle strangulation in its amorous embrace : pusillanimous prudence advises him to take flight, but the passion of the hunt wins out and makes the fear of death almost sweet : this passion represents a higher form of military exercise and packs caution off to hell : stubborn and tireless he will tame the animal again using his mastery of ritual wisdom, exploring the remaining undiscovered crannies in its lair, longing to make the most of his ministry, like those souls who so thirst after perfection and scrupulously prolong the recitation of their prayers long after their devotions are at an end : adoration will continue all night, and the following day, when twilight comes, the spartan cycle will begin anew

9

you will subject geography to the imperatives and demands of your passion : from the backstreets of Riad Ez-Zitoun to the vicinity of the Gare du Nord, you set out the elements of the backdrop that will frame your hosts : the sibylline snake charmer in Djemaa el Fna summons tourists and natives with his rhythmic drumming and you join the circle of spectators, taking no pains to disguise your emotion : you have slowly stripped away the habits and principles you were taught from childhood : you were a mismatch : like a snake sloughing off its skin, you abandoned them by the wayside and went on walking : your body gained sinuous ophidian slipperiness and the mere sighting of enemy fauna stirs up sumptuous images of verbal violence : your contact will be the knife : the piercing scream of the queen tottering through the station lobby creates a sacred space around her that shuts out bystanders alien to her delirium and, following her example, you will melt your own invulnerability into brusque defiance of their logic : you couldn't care less about their world's future and no humanitarian considerations will suborn your conscience : don't trust yourself : ditching face, name, family customs, and country is not enough : ascesis must proceed : each word in your language likewise is out to trap you : from now on you will learn to think against your own language

10

once more you descend into the crypt : the inexorable rage against your old flock and pleasure at witnessing her offensive burlesque will encourage you to hustle and bustle through the dark tumult down the passage on your way to non-gold bearing shrines that aren't remotely revolutionary : shimmying, furiously fanning themselves because of the heat or turning up the lapels of their furs, shivering violently from the cold, hysterically chit-chatting, powdering their noses, tidying their hair, tittering, gargling, sighing, the members of the order converse next to their hieratic guards while they wait anxiously for their prince : their extreme brassiness is a clear reaction to the tribe's no less extreme repression : a centrifugal force greater than the vulgar law of gravity that launched them like errant meteorites into this distant underground basilica : shards from the Cádiz explosion, spread by the four winds, summoned there by quirk of fate! : they find the solo flautist beguiling and dedicate their devotions to him : look at the lovelies : their temerity knows no bounds : they race frantically through their antiphons, communions and orations like people who know they're sentenced to die at dawn and are desperate to suck life dry : more than four centuries of stigma and disgrace, prison, torture and the stake (from the time of the frigid queen's savage spiteful decree and the autos-de-fe unleashed by her grotesque offspring) have shaped the endemic tension setting them apart from the other activists of the guild : corpses strung out on a Hitlerian ghetto scale (bundles of firewood, sambenitos, muzzles, white scapulars, flaming conical caps), their delirious provocation spreads to every jurisdiction in the world : centuries-old atavism drives them to theatrical exaggeration and hyperbole when they huffily confection the character of the sad royal imprisoned in Tordesillas : a JuandeOrduñesque victim of love : in the grandiloquent performance by the film's star actress : concealing in a limp-handed flurry of gestures her king's vacant stillness : the beautiful flamingo, white plumage in front, blood red at the back, reproduced in color prints in the usual school textbook : hot-blooded biped vertebrate, a heart complete with auricles and ventricles, a strong swimmer and, according to his mood, a lover of the nest or fugitive thereof : back to the wall, like others of his ilk, displaying calculated contempt : nasal orifices, penetrating beady little eyes, a possibly toothless mouth, a cigarette in its beak-holder : broken-winged, long-legged, seemingly resting on one leg while occasionally gathering up the other and indolently resting its sole on holes in the plaster or crev-

63

ices in the wall : and with the silent consent of guards and court-
iers, Aurora hardly Borealis accelerates her lunatic gesticulating,
wrapped in the halo of admiration and pity for her splendiferous-
tragic fate : her eyes sparkle cheekily behind the light black veil,
her caked make-up flakes and runs derisorily round the corners
of her lips : lifting an outstretched index finger, she will mutter a
thousand and one times that the king is not dead, that he has but
fallen asleep : using the very peculiar diction of that pleiad of imi-
tators who, fleeing the rigors of the country, blossom a thousand
leagues away, in some humble recondite place : history is sometimes just and the Catholic mother will contemplate the raw spectacle in horror : vengeance wrought by the hated brother and his
vilified friends : the scene is repeated daily without chronicle or
bard and the almighty power of your modest craft stuns you : the
drag queens' ghostly soliloquies will revenge the memory of the
king : abruptly, you annihilate centuries of infamy with a mere
squiggle of your pen

11

MAIS DIEU CREA LES ARABES
you are
he said textually
the best known among all men, you command what's just, you for-
bid what's unjust and you believe in me
textually in the pages of the book lent by a colleague, after one of
your regular rendezvous down one of the asphalt avenues in the
every day less Luminous City

and the love you will find with them will be as burning and barren as the desert plains : far from the damp mossy grottoes sheltering the nocturnal movement of water underground : all is limpid here : supple muscular bodies their distant sinuous enfolding suggesting the bare convexity of dunes : when the dust storm blurs their obtuse shapes and the simoom's flaming breath completes the task of foreshortening and suffuses the tawny landscape with rapid animal panting : curves and yet more curves imbricated in powering waves, promiscuous communal coupling, elastic, never contorted simultaneity of tensions and embraces in the hot malleable weft : ripples snaking over vibratile skin, delicately sculpting sober masterly lines : no femine artifice or embellishment : no flowerbeds, orchards, arbors, dainty laughing meadows : muscle and stone : broken, corroded and eroded by the wind's sustained action : no seminal rain to fertilize it : dry, dry! : greenery is an effort and a prize : the trunk of the solitary palm tree signals the invisible presence of the well, though you will not drink from there : drinking one's fill like the crowd repels you : the sturdy sprig from the tree will demolish their outdated laws, with bastard pride you will slowly slake your thirst : its bitter sap will do you : let the dogs bark and bark : the caravan passes : again the desert invites you, vast and tenacious as your desire, and you will go deep into the massive configuration of its implacable coppery chest : hilly arms wall the line of the horizon, mercifully isolate you from the hostile fertile world : step by step across the shield of its smooth abdomen you will reach the nearest oasis thanks to the fine instinct of the meharis : Anselm Turmeda, Père de Foucauld, Lawrence of Arabia? : among your own at last, immersed in their thick human stew, barely recognizable under graying beard and dust-covered filthy garb : your sunglasses protect you and hide your lynx's eyes from curious zealous gazes : your eyes have lost the bland sweetness of adolescence and the maniacal glare searching out the whereabouts of prey will upset the peace of mind of any rash Nazarene who dares spy on them : the Muslim out of Christianity and now raging through the souks of Africa is the negation of the order ruling his world and he will point an accusing finger at you : his gawky silhouette is a deception, a severe prophylaxis is warranted : dreg, outlaw, renegade, sodomite, pervert? : worse, much worse! : he is a sower of winds : and as the proverb says

12

whoever sows winds, reaps tempests
uttered a thousand times by cautious measured throats, the warn-
    ing will not reach the escapees from your species driven by cen-
    trifugal forbidden passion to these arid stony shores
the baritones of the old order thunder in vain from the pulpits of
    their committees, institutes and churches and, armed with the
    precise dart of the word, you take mocking aim at the mastheads
    of their obese respectability and the sweep and swollen lines of
    their sodden self-righteousness
against their spirit of authority and hierarchy, based on prohibi-
    tions and laws you will pit an egalitarian generic subversion of a
    naked upstanding body
the cock, you got it, the cock
the sturdy stem channeling sap to its head!
laughter will be your crossbow

with its wild corrosive help, you will puncture their fatuous bal-
loons and expose their petty derisory fear to the realities of the
world
one by one
you pluck off their pathetic masks
bird in the hand
but not neglecting those in the bush
you will also force them to strip and subject them to the cruel
ridicule of your avenging discourse
listen carefully to what we say
the traps set by your logic won't catch us
morality
religion
society
patriotism
family
are threatening noises and their sonorous clatter leave us indifferent
don't count on us
we believe in a world without frontiers
wandering Jews
heirs to John Lackland
we'll set up camp where our instinct takes us
the Agarene community attracts us so we'll take refuge there
forget that same old story
the ancient hackneyed threat of shameful ruin and catastrophe
après nous le déluge?
WE SHALL SOW TEMPESTS!

III

not like now

when pent-up blinkered rage spills into the closed precincts of basements and police cells, physical humiliation of the hatedfeared beings (unconscious objects of their envy and maybe of hidden desire), repeated beatings, assaults on the phantoms of their own anguish (a continuously frustrated exorcism, however), stifled screams of the victims and contented grunts of uniformed proboscides (viciously loudmouthing each other on), sale race dégueulasse pouilleux ordure saloperie (modulated in the language of Villon and Descartes), futile attempts at answering back (perhaps a clumsy dash for it), sudden decision by the mastiff-in-chief to flourish his revolver (invoking legitimate self-defense), customary regulation cry of halt (shouted three times), shots blasting, confusion, yelling, panic of the mastodons, frantic rallying of witnesses, sequence of differing accounts, emphatic press communiqués, contradictions that stick out a mile, pointed questions that remain unanswered, prickly embarrassed silence

on the grand scale then

when the filthy hounds of the L'Allergie Française openly imposed their law on the streets (blanket friskings, massive roundups, discriminatory curfews) and dozens upon dozens of manacled corpses (bullet holes in temples or necks bruised from strangulation) floated to the surface down the river beautifully celebrated by the poets, under those same bridges evoked by chansonniers to mournful tunes from accordions and guitars (meanwhile the local council was voting the budget necessary to feed the pigeons and wash down public buildings and monuments, and children's happy chatter filled the city's lovely parks and gardens), at the precise moment that your implacable hatred of your own marks of identity (race profession class family nation) was growing, you felt yourself being pulled magnetically towards the pariahs at a similar rate, and the violence wrought in the name of the civilizing mission (to which, on the outside, you still belonged) deepened the abyss between them and you and reinforced the sense of betrayal and deviation nestling eagle-like in your breast, when with a feeling of proud solidarity you observed their serried ranks emerge defiantly from metro exits only to be kicked and gun-butted into the black holes of police vans and as there weren't enough of these, lined up, arms raised behind necks, on the vast sidewalks of that place de l'Étoile that tout à coup était devenue jaune, reviving the humiliation of a ghetto from less than a quarter of a century ago

but back again now

not in the intricate labyrinth of passages and tunnels perhaps designed by a sickly mole in his insomniac delirium in Prague (the shrill squeaking of automatic doors shutting, NICOLAS FINES BOUTEILLES repeated at a deranged frequency on stairs, maps showing the bus lines, safety notices nobody reads, adverts for DU BO DU BON DUBONNET glimpsed in the sudden rush of light from passing trains, tempting offers hawked by a prosperous consumer society with its vast range of makes of car, package holidays, toilet paper that almost caresses your skin, wondrous cheeses, sublime elixirs, underwear mouthwatering or just for papa, benevolent loan-granting banking institutions arrayed against a background

69

of picture-postcard landscapes, happy couples and sexy girls, when the long abolished May's lively spirit of invention splattered walls with sarcastic cynical comic fierce insolent doubting hilarious graffiti, introducing corrosive seeds of destruction into the aforesaid polychrome self-indulgence, only to be followed by the subsequent predictable resurge of hallowed values, favoring the malign obtuse rancor of the, alas!, not always silent majority, the moral outrage of the average clean-living citizen, the expansive gesture of a pale Eurocrat hand, beyond all suspicion, sketching in pencil, paint or red lipstick the somber images tormenting his sleep

MORT AUX BOUGNOLS

RATONS = SYPHILIS

UNE FEMME QUI COUCHE AVEC UN ARABE EST PIRE QU'UNE PUTAIN)

out, out

when the annual summer blood-letting (exudation?) has cleared the urban arteries of their manufactured toxins and the bloated city regains its pristine nubile figure for a few weeks : a remarkable August slimming routine inviting one to enjoy open views of the body without fat or varicose veins and enticing the lone foreigner loitering in the rearguard to engage in an exciting new itinerary : not the usual cityscape of the ubiquitous masses in motion : the anonymous neutral faces of the hydra with infinite heads : the setting rather for an old thirties film of lovers kissing by a metro entrance : pensioners sitting on park benches, idle strollers, a harmless Salvation Army choir, maybe a peaceful game of pétanque : the mist spirals down over the empty boulevard, and, forsaken by its own, the city suddenly belongs to you, to you and those foreign bastards (far from gregarious sun worshippers, family campers cheek by jowl on campsites, faked tans, lizards prostrate by the poolside, the lethargic child-producing brigade, cars careering like light tanks)

slowly, you make for the public-works trench that, like an airplane's death trail, has gutted the tarmac and spread wide the earth, uncovered the entire stretch parallel to a plank walkway put in place for pedestrians where you'll venture now as the humble sappers toil at your feet with pick and shovel and a distant juddering drill perforates your eardrums with its monotone rat-a-tat-tat : de-surplus-valued blacks of the common trench, in direct contact with filth, vile discharge, viscerally plebeian excretions : long before your aborted birth into the lap of a virtuous reputable family? : at the imperious bidding of an overseer, as in Great-grandfather's glory days? : foul recurrent nightmare, its indelible stigma stubbornly pursuing you despite your unflagging protracted efforts to throw it off : the virginal page offers delightful new scope for redemption and the added thrill of profaning its whiteness : a mere squiggle of the pen will suffice : you will create their bodies anew impelled by the violent passion they arouse, never concealing its truth in threadbare linear descriptions or destroying their masterful presence via illusory naming operations : committing their physical existence to paper thanks to a sumptuous proliferation of signs and exuberant accumulation of figures of speech : using all the tricks of your rhetorical trade : tropes, synecdoche, metonyms, metaphors : taxing to the limit the sinews of each phrase, entangling them in contagious copulations, struggling might and main with elusive words : knotted tightly, clasping vines, you follow meekly out of the corner of your eye, as eagerly submissive as the complement escorting a verb! : scaling the trunk, past blossoming fleshy lips and on to the hirsute foliage of a Babylonian hanging garden : gripping your pen, forcing the seminal fluid to spurt, holding it erect on the blank page : abrupt syncopated movements : plenitude and genesis between your hands : their heads sticking out of the trench level with your shoes and your gaze lingers there, a tame prey to their animal allure : no urban haze can dull their glow : no work clothes can disguise the radiant quality of sons of the desert : bodies set in the rigor and harshness of their beliefs, bound to their instinct for life as to a plain irrefutable axiom, you allow their presence to make its case with the blinding clarity of an aphorism : gradually become inebriated on their nomad spirit, their burning salutary solar essence : independent and free like a Bedouin chieftain : master of air, wind, and light, of the vast spaces and immense void : above, the subtle colorless sky, below, the sand, pure as a gleaming glacier

identifying with that stubborn Stylites who, scorning worldly fame, withdrew to inaccessible heights in pursuit of higher perfection : twenty-seven years resisting the teasing smiling ambivalent devil trying every wile of flesh-and-blood flirtation : balancing one-footed atop his column with the pomp and ceremony of a diurnal fowl, a mere few inches from the cunning treacherous tempter : ignoring his smile's fatal attraction, the cool lascivious attentions of his huge flickering tongue : arms splayed heavenwards, lips immersed in prayer : but that distant solitary peak offers you secret rewards and your apparent lunacy is fully justified : the diameter and length of the column's shaft, the cylindrical polished surface serving as your prop would be enough to meet King Kong's devoted flock's wildest dreams of bliss : add in the ecstasies and epiphanies from the spectacle on high and penitence will be transformed into a hallowed garden of delights : no hermit he : a sybarite : virtuous in the eyes of the world yet verily surrendering to the joys of uncharted nocturnal devotion to the attributes of your savage master

sexual roots of political power : or political roots of sexual power : exercise of absolute dominion at any rate over inert insensitive bodies, express or tacit accomplices of an arbitrary all-intrusive will : contemptuous manipulation of beings stripped of all traces of humanity whose shouts of tighten-the-screw long-live-our-chains reinforce the illusion of a staged ceremony of renunciation of their own destinies : docile embrace of their condition as objects : hidden foundations of the ominous notion of Power : subjugating castrating reptilian presence, images of coercion secreted into the hidden depths of the soul accompanying Caesar in his rise and fall : destructive monolithic tyranny going far back in time, you tell yourself, like a story that is never ending

up river or down : ascent or descent : at the self-absorbed rhythm of the sail zigzagging adroitly between specious natural scenarios : humble shacks, yawning caves, forest of palms, slowly rippling canebrakes : as if trapped in a grim recurrent nightmare : past landscapes from old photographs in the mansion, along shadowy passages, at the twilight dawn of your childhood : images fusing in your memory at the speed of a magic lantern and you will join the polyglot party, striving to conceal your emotions : ruins, ruins, babelian archeology, baritone cicerone chattering ad nauseam : in the vast panorama of hats, cine cameras, tourist guides, tinted glasses of groups wending and un-wending their way under the protection of massive lofty columns : the turbaned guard beckons furtively and, abandoning the promiscuous throng, you decide to follow in his footsteps : white flash of a smile sealing a conniving silent accord, necessary preamble for your meander in the dark! : the flickering candle flame lights up his hand's dancing silhouette as you slither through tunnels and galleries : his compact body cast into relief by his tempting swirling djellaba, thick bushy eyebrows enhancing the twinkle in his eye : tenors and mezzos still declaiming up above names dates facts that flow with slick erudition, a musical counterpoint accompanying you as you go down, down and down into Pluto's gloomy realm : happy to see off the inevitable troupe of troubadours, all doublets and feathered hats : the unseemly outburst of bel canto slowly fading into the background : attentive only to your mentor's feline moves : plunging further and further, witness to your own vertiginous fall : his body's textual subversion silencing the vapid speechifying, and the diva's final tremolo, a gasp between the gaping jaws of cavernous mastiff : your present unfettered happiness is that of a man damned : the whirlpool has sucked you to the bottom : you know, now you know : you will never climb back out

imagine you're up among your old fauna : ruddy-cheeked pillar of the illustrious local establishment, string-pulling magnate of a distinguished overseas consortium, medallioned pachyderm on a pompous executive committee, smiling archangel in a remote fiscal paradise : signed up perhaps with extras resurrected from your childhood to an elite management course for industrialists : cloistered with them in a neo-Gothic lecture-theatre in some primly elegant university institution in Massachusetts : the VIPs memorizing the sublime advice from the computer, deciding to implement it diligently, slavishly and promptly : to sign the letter firing their firm's longest-serving employee, without taking into account his selfless work record or horrific family circumstances, and go to bed and sleep the whole night through untroubled by scruples or remorse : young Turk at last, deployer of capital and lives, promoter of enterprises and initiatives, practical wise engineer of souls! : all the glittering prizes inherent in your new status : credit cards, jet travel, gear and tackle advertised in the color pages of *L'Express*, red coupé with wifey smoking in its upholstered interior : dreaming about climbing higher, ever higher and camping out in the arctic solitudes at the top : proving your mettle as a valiant captain of industry thanks to tests more arduous than any Carnegian course in New England : eliminating your own begetter now worn out by use and transformed into a source of pointless losses, chucking him unceremoniously down the pan : mentally relishing the savings from such an audacious entrepreneurial move, you vigorously pull the chain : the world's great and the good will recognize and admire you as one of their own : you will never, but never, alight on the platform : driving the powerful engine of their miraculous technical revolution, the train would take you, oh dear, so very dear Herr Álvaro Krupp, to the far ends of the world

but the subsoil of Africa will do for you as you follow the ritual of the suras, hanging on the seer's lips, surrendering yourself to his sonorous spell with raw savage joy

oh infidels
I do not worship whom you worship
you do not worship whom I worship
I will not worship whom you worship
you will not worship whom I worship
keep to your religion, I have my own!

the tenor voices, with their trills and tremolos, sully the limpid recitation of prayers, and the hoity-toity Europeans will get their massive injection of culture bawled at them at quite an inordinate pitch
: poco a poco s'indebolì l'autorità centrale e, nel corso del secondo
interregno, vi fù l'invasione degli : : "at the end of a shaft hewn
into the rock" : or : ce n'est qu'à l'avènement de la onzième dynastie,
originaire de Thèbes, que l'empire : or even : die Könige des Neuen
Reiches werden in Tal der Königsgraber zu Theben begraben : until
the different choirs rush into the sibyl where you've both taken refuge, and seeing the abject spectacle, sink into pregnant silence
(POSSIBLE REACTIONS

they turn a blind eye
their faces change color
they clear their throats or cough
cross themselves
speak of moral corruption)

from zero hours earlier today onward you will proclaim yourself in
a state of love with the Nubians : serried ranks of their bodies besiege
you meld into the black of night and defensive-offensive operations
are unleashed at a dizzy rate following the conventional strategy of
a blitzkrieg : assiduous reader of von Clausewitz that you are, you

will painstakingly pursue your ends with the methodical precision of a monocled member of the Prussian General Staff : conjecturing where their power resides as they viciously flourish swift sharp-pointed spears : backs tensely arched ready to target you with their arrows, threatening to make you bristle like a hedgehog : grappling in a series of man-to-man combats, your predatory claws holding them down till they're disarmed : you have exchanged a fertile land of gardens and meadows for one bounded by hedges of thorns : the aridity of the steppes banishes the very idea of fruit and you are entranced by the brazen barrenness : your amorous imperialism knows no bounds and, like a fire-drake, basilisk or phantasmagorical beast, you quench your aching thirst in the relentless give and take of the contest : no reprieve, truce or quarter given! : in turn taming their stubborn pride and lingeringly savoring their rough attentions : felucca boatmen riding the river's greased muscles or swarthy hillsmen subjugating enemy territory : not forgetting the nubile innocence of a boy unafraid of the lunging beast : prolonging the skirmishes and encounters that lead gradually to your goal : to the delights of willing submission : "to the servitude summoning you with its unwholesome glamour" : the voice of the reader of the Koran chanting his rosary of suras reaches the dingy room where you lie in a haze of kef : insatiable, you advance the incursions of your holy war across the entire country

almighty powers of the written word!
with a mere pad of paper and a couple of uncapped ballpoints (one's ink ran out barely a minute ago, its generative strength exhausted), confined to the tiny room where you usually work (a

kitchen adapted for the concoction of your strange recipes), with a polyglot guide to the country and a blurred portrait of your alter ego as your only aids you've launched off (and will launch off whoever reads you), drifting on the gentle tide, inspired by a puff of wind, have admired the double row of sphinxes pockmarked by cameras from sightseeing tours, attended a short course for managing directors held five thousand leagues away, recited Allahu Akbar hands on knees and torso horizontal to the ground, made love blind, followed speechifying cicerone on customs at the court of the Pharaoh, smoked a pipe of kef on a boatman's welcoming bolster, his arts of persuasion stretching to all those willingly caught in his nets, momentarily forgetting their dismally wretched lives : yours is a singular civilization, condemned to live by proxy! : producer and consumers marked by the same indelible stigma, like different players in an identical game : at once exhibitionists and peeping toms

I/YOU
impersonal pronouns, empty substantive shells! : your scant reality is the speech act by which you appropriate language and submit it to the deceptive control of your malleable subjectivity : empty wineskins, cellars at the ready, you offer yourselves up for promiscuous general use and collective social enjoyment : nuclear hermetic indicatives, nonetheless you pass on your uniqueness when with a mere squiggle of my pen I make you all jump to the diktats of my changing protean voices : the frequencies you broadcast over favor subtle sleights of hand, beyond ordinary communication : who's expressing himself as I/you? : the shades wandering in your

indispensable emptiness transmute, and you can skillfully play with signs your naïve reader doesn't notice : immersing him in an unstable world, prey to a continuous process of destruction : assigning your scattered egos, the different parts in the choir, at the behest of the virtuoso flight of your baton : the pen gently running over the blank rectangle of the page

a jester's bawdy arts call for oneiric transformation and with a seer's accomplished flair, you will decide the ritual order in which the scene must be staged : embodying in turn the happenstance of contradictory impulses that govern human activity : simultaneous desire for absolute control and annihilation in the act of self-surrender : dictator and martyr in one : cadaver in the service of whatever cause and forger of destinies and lives depending on the pulsing of your will : exorcising demons in bloody ludic confrontation, your only weapon naked discourse : transforming violence into sign : sweeping its loathsome face from the earth : converting it into a pretext for verbal jousting

IV

PAULO MAIORA CANAMUS

from the vast latitudes of space to the equally vast latitudes of time : from school atlases of the world to old history textbooks : barely recovered from an oneiric razzia through the phantom orb of north Africa and ready now, helped only by pen and paper, for a fresh unpredictable expedition into the Einsteinian fourth dimension : cloistered, as always, in your tiny room : not forsaking the area of your own writing : focusing your interest on the exemplary trajectory of the country that has ceased to be yours and means merely this to you now : a convenient staging post on the road to Africa : boardinghouse, inn, place of transit : a stain on the map : thanks to the collection of documents piled high on your shelves, almost within arm's reach : irrefutable evidence of incorrigible tenacity in the pursuit of self-mutilation and punishment extended over centuries with a hard grit worthy of a better cause : from the era when, as an impish charmer of the fauna once observed, the now-unified Peninsula was an area populated by a variety of corrupt many-colored beings, a shameful past to be hidden from sight, from the lives of leprous lunatic or syphilitic forebears to the purest bravest stripling from the Meseta the moment he was preparing to spill his blood so generously on behalf of the perpetuation of the kingdom of Seneca, a lugubrious era with differing beliefs, freedom of expression, illicit passions, a time when the

Christian king himself dressed in the Moorish style and endorsed by example the crimine pessimo, outrageous behavior that finally provoked the righteous reaction of his sister the queen, memorably clearing the terrain for a pruning of condemned rotten limbs from the nation's vigorous thriving trunk, hundreds of thousands, nay millions, of brutish lethargic effeminate beings fond of bestial entertainments and totally in thrall to carnal vices that, when their presence ceased to offend the pure of blood, transformed that people of tillers of the glebe into a learned conclave of theologians and the libidinous country of the Archpriest into an austere and solemn passion play, a great theater of the world where the mass of the audience identified individual dignity with total immobility of the mind and fanatically attended the ritual execution of reprobates, Judaizers, sodomites, bigamists and Lutherans who invoked a tolerance that, as Menéndez Pelayo said, is but the weakness and castrated logic of the eunuch, and tried to spread to the healthy part of the country perverse extravagant doctrines and execrable filthy vices, thus establishing a soul-saving intransigence and obstinacy that, beyond our frontiers, would earn us hatred and hostility, repeated slanders, relentless phobias, as our military genius extended our Empire's glorious borders to the very ends of the universe, an unbending attitude toward life sustained over four centuries, in the teeth of severe reverses and setbacks, defeats, attacks and disasters, finally becoming a genuine exercise in ascesis, by dint of which the gradual intervention of antibodies has spared our organism the lethal load of toxins that today poisons societies with less foresight than our own, confronting them with the terrible dilemma of slow death by strangulation or cruel most painful amputation the charmer's voice gradually silenced yours and you listen to his monotonous deadpan discourse while, from the books piled around your table, on the ramshackle filing cabinet, in your tiniest of libraries, other anxious frantic discordant voices call out and unleash themselves upon you, demand their turn, their inalienable right to be heard, denied for years, decades, centuries, from the black solitude of dungeon or rack, the gloomy silence of a household perpetually besieged by informers or the rabble's lurid cries around the bundles of firewood, stifled extinguished voices, the hidden history of thousands and thousands of fellow ex-countrymen, who didn't succeed in escaping like you, a history never told, buried in the sanctuaries of their ever-profane consciences, experienced in grisly contest with a surly cast of ponderous or solemn or frenzied convulsed and grotesque upstarts, hidalgos and conquistadors, nobles and inquisitors, virgins and whores, picaroons and squires, the people, the people, a petrified enchanted sleeping-beauty society that, from the days of poor Joan the Mad to those of sterile Charles the Bewitched, he of the jutting jaw, agreed, expressly or tacitly expeditious, to the measures enforced without appeal by a stout instrument of repression intent on creating an impermeable hermetic cordon sanitaire around the baleful country, betrayals, confessions, trials, confiscations of property, recantations, damnations, burning of books and documents, of apostates, Jews, heretics, adepts of that nefast sin that, though exposed to public shaming, still merited the pious attentions of a Quevedo's witty muse, history never lived yet killed to death, a demented epic, a funereal song of war, intoned against a shifting backdrop of processions, comic routines, plays, bullfights, sporting events, catchy operettas, sound and fury, Ravel's interminable bolero, empty hollow gestures, pro-

longed across the centuries, with no real continuity, pure historical inertia, until the other was born, he who was you, into the heart of an atrophied bourgeoisie out of step with time, some forty years ago, as yet another unwilling bit-player in a bilious bloody saga, three years of frenzy, destruction and pillaging, bitter civil conflict, infamous slaughter of a million compatriots, crowning masterpiece of a nation where, if by chance you linger, you do so only because you happen to be passing through, clamorous dissident voices insistently demand your attention, invite you to hold out your arm, pick up the book or volume where they are to be found, to glance painfully over the pages and hear their testimony to times when, as the liberated Poet wrote, their congenital lack of reason, madness today, was enforced as an admirable paradox
but forever listening
listening
until that wonderful epiphany we all remember, when relentless internal subversion, with foreign aid, tried to abolish marriage and the family, subordinate the spiritual to the material, impose committees, not brotherhoods, to bonnet our beloved Giralda in dirty astrakhan caps, a destructive enterprise that though conclusively defeated on the field of battle now persists with its spirit-sapping endeavors via new more subtle means, trying to succeed peacefully where force of arms failed, through corruption of intellects, eroticism, pornography, degenerate spectacles, sick filthy literature that likes to insult our patriotic and political ideals, trying to pollute the country with drugs, blurred sexual roles, proliferation of sordid dance-halls, a lethal threat to our luminous future, our most noble holy patrimony, against which we must defend ourselves, if necessary, tooth and nail, and nip in the bud what our sworn enemies are

attempting. namely, the creation of an effeminate impressionable youth that may be destroyed one day by the sudden eruption of cruel macho hordes from the East

ANIMUS MEMINISSE HORRET

it all began in the baths
when the Infante Don Sancho did perishe in the great catastrophie in Zalaca, the king summoned his wysemen and bishops to discover whyye his belycose knights were e're softe, and they did replie strait because they oft visited the publick baths and did surrender to th' unbrydled appetytes and fraylties of the fleshe

>and it be no wise too notorious and palpable an example that I do wishe to examyne in th' dishonest, vyle, filthie, and horrible sinne of fornycation and eville coupling as it doth fall outside the riyte matrimonie God's commandments hath ordained, th' infinite harm that today befalleth the bodie and the soul e'er on the fact that he who giveth himself up to such excesses of carnal delectation doth lose his appetyte for foodde and even feel a burning thyrste when toping, for amour and lycense bringeth on many maladies and curtaileth the lives of men, ayging and greying before tyme, their limbs shaketh, their five senses fadeth, and they do even shed some in parte or whollie and hence are to blame for the enfeeblement of human bodies, and thence men do become listless at arms and other contestes, are palsyied, jew-hearted, broken redes, and weke

and as in present tymes our sinnes multiplie incessantlie
and bad habyts continueth unabayted and as the most
common sinne be disorderlie loving in the baths, which
causeth dysputation, foundlings, murderie, scandalls, and
even perdition of propertie and perdition of persons, and,
worse, the perdition of errant souls synce the abominable appetytes of the fleshe spurne nothing and oft lovers
do not seek femayles yet do lust after the companye of
mayles to wreke their foull deeds, men to do such acts
with who are womennish in their deedes and little femayles in their perverse desyres, that it dost seem th' ende of
the world is nigh, cause no feyre of God nor of his thunder existeth and people have no shayme, and th' earth and
heavens shoulde quake and absolve people of this kynde in
bodie and soul as evill beestes, animals faute of good sense,
brainne, reasonne and understanding in their horrible
works and sodomite acts, all sinnes that because of the
baths visit upon our realmes grete harm and confusyon,
the publick goodde demandeth they be shutte and laide
wayste herewithe, and please Our Lord the Almightie, Je-
sus Christ, the Incarnate, Firstborne, begat by the word
of God the Father in the virgynal wombe of the holie and
blessèd Mother, so we may see and perceive that and pro-
tecte ourselves from Satan our enemie, and turn our
backes on vices and sinnes and change for the better, so
we be worthie of entering with Him in that beautiful invi-
tation to the blessed matrimonie in the glories of paradyse
forever and ever amen

DE VITA ET MORIBUS

yes, OUR COUNTRY IS DIFFERENT
this expression, popular today around the globe thanks to provident lavish campaigns by our consulates and tourist agencies, is more than a successful publicity slogan and into the bargain speaks to an undeniable reality only fools or the blind would dare question : what other country, apart from ours, could in fact offer a traveler folklore so rich in its customs and practices that they will find nothing like it in the five corners of the world : what other nation, apart from ours, could present the curious visitor, eager for new sensations and strong emotions, such colorful lively and original entertainments as the ones he can witness for free every Sunday and holiday, after complying with the teachings of Our Holy Mother Church, in the squares and arenas of the main cities on the Peninsula : extraordinary dépaysement, tremendous break from it all, transporting him our traveler thousands of leagues away while he watches, entranced, the preparations for our most unique, most national fiesta! : a gloomy yet gleeful ceremony, an incomparable ritual of life and death that enraptures the most serene souls and warrants the liturgical atmosphere, the devoted attention of countless familiars, advisers and fans who month in month out pack the balconies and terraces : while the powers-that-be and the great and the good parade in their finest frippery, squeeze into the president's box and stand in their soutanes and birettas, combat gear, medals, combs, and mantillas : moments of restrained emotion and silent expectation allowing our sensual though chaste females slowly and surely to practice their bewitching hieratic flirtation! : resourceful inspired language of suggestion, glances, pouts and playful fanning

: not without humane compassionate tenderness welling in their large dark eyes, sultanas or Pharaoh's spouses, when the actors and bit-players in the drama sweep majestically into the square to the loud hurrahs of the spectators : constables, judges, inquisitors, the condemned, the presiding Father, those relaxed to secular tribunals : the prisoners dressed and adorned in the traditional manner chez nous, with the usual distinctive garments and impedimenta : sambenitos, painted cones, gags, white or yellow habits, boxed in by wooden planks, depending on their status or holed up in a kind of coffin, or else wearing a grotesque crooked cornet and riding on the back of a burro : even though the ceremony has its strict rules, habitués and foreign aficionados will always find, we can guarantee, that element of subtle improvisation which ensures the rite's perpetual novelty : some proceed to the auto with aplomb, dignity and sangfroid and when their gags are lifted minutes before the bonfire's lit passionately recite a psalm : others recant at the last minute and by virtue of their sincere if tardy recantations, are let off with a garroting : a third group, swayed by the preacher's persuasive rhetoric, goes silent and with a noble expiatory gesture humbly place the bundles of firewood on their own heads : contemptuous of exhortations by confessors and judges, others stick stubbornly to their syllogisms and errors, indifferent to the preparations set in train by the executioner and the rabble's jeers and insults : the motives for the crime and consequent punishment also vary, thus avoiding monotonous repetition of more of the same, giving the auto a surprise factor that, as you will have experienced personally, keeps the audience on its toes, forcing it to hold its breath until the grand finale : yesterday the tourists who came to see the beautiful monuments of our unrivalled Andalusian capital, on their return from a pleasantly instructive visit to the famous bodegas in Jerez, were uniquely privileged to witness an auto-de-fe in the old plaza de San Francisco, honored by the presence of the Bishops of the Canary Islands and Lugo, the Cathedral Council, the Royal Council, the Duchess of Béjar, numerous illustrious ladies, and an endless throng of knights and yeomen, when twenty-one Lutherans were relaxed by the secular arm and another eighty were sentenced to the pillory and publicly denounced : the day before yesterday, Club Med members witnessed a solemn burning, in Madrid, of fifty men convicted of the nefast sin : a jester, one of Count Villamediana's boys-in-waiting, a young mulatto slave, another of Villamediana's servants and a page from the Duke of Alba's retinue : ladies and damsels took pity on their extreme youth and ill-used ways and there were moments of high emotion when the executioner tied the very young contrite page to the stake and, scowling, lit the bonfire : of course, we are only too conscious of the fact that the blatant ferocity of this harsh virile spectacle runs the risk of momentarily upsetting some spectators, especially members of the fairer sex who have voyaged from afar : and our tourist guides and brochures thus recommend that delicate or over-impressionable individuals should abstain : the initial shock might be too much and we wouldn't want a negative experience to blot the hopefully happy memories of their holidays in our hospitable and sunny country : for these ladies we surely have a vast array of other diversions and entertainments to delight : but we can have no truck whatsoever with the obsessive harping campaign in one sector of the foreign press that regularly proclaims us to be brutes and bores moaning on about our "barbaric ways" : such hypocritical humanitarianism, worthy of menopausal spinsters or the Lady President of the Royal

Society for the Protection of Animals, doesn't take into account the complex eminently cathartic character of our expiatory exemplary fiesta : to truly understand the auto-de-fe, one has to grasp it as a tragic redemptive total experience : naturally, the spectacle of a man burnt to cinders at the stake may seem at first sight an intolerable atrocity : but if we consider the gravity of the act he is accused of, such a terrible death agony has its positive compensatory side, which, even in cases of the greatest abjection and vileness, endows the executed with an enviable aura of dignity : the convulsions, the screams, the stench of burnt flesh are merely elements accompanying the tragedy and only the real auto enthusiast can properly appreciate them : examining them not in isolation but as fully integrated within an overall global image of the event : as the distinguished author of *Death in the Afternoon* has noted (as familiar with our fiesta as Lope de Vega!), an audience addicted to burnings at the stake possesses an innately tragic sense of life, thanks to which it views and values the secondary features of the spectacle in terms of the whole : and this tragic sense is something as personal and random as having or not having an ear for music : because as the main impression a listener without the latter will take away from a symphony concert will be the one created by the gestures and movements of the double-bass player, a spectator at an auto will only recall the painful agony of those being relaxed : but their convulsions and howls, when judged in isolation, lack any real meaning : if an audience member takes the same humanitarian spirit to his symphony that he applies to his autos, he will find an equally huge field for his charitable and benevolent desires : he can dream of improving the salaries and conditions of bass players, as he would have liked to chip in on behalf of those condemned to the redeeming bonfire : but if he is in full possession of his faculties and knows symphony orchestras must be valued as a whole and heard in their entirety, he will probably react only with pleasure, approval and joy : he won't assess the double bass in isolation from the orchestra and won't think of the criminal, not for a fraction of a second, as a human individual who is thinking, suffering, writhing and screaming

FINIS CORONAT OPUS

and what about the executed?, you will say : aren't they human beings like everyone else? : or don't heretics, sinners and members of the ranks of the unclean degenerate castes suffer? : and although the best doctors and scientific authorities are unanimous in finding that depraved men and individuals from bastard or diseased races do not have the same sensitivity to pain as right-minded pure-blooded folk, we will for the moment ignore that argument in order to concentrate on the immense benefits that accrue to the condemned as a result of their torture : because, my beloved children, why do you think we tied you to the stake if it was not to redeem you through suffering and show you the hard flinty path to Christian salvation? : don't then curse the punishments you face : your bodies will be charred and reduced to ash : but you will have souls that are free to fly, by virtue of genuine repentance, to the happy eternal dwelling-place of the chosen : that's why we subject you to the water-torture, the rack, insomnia, the hood, the hot bricks and lead you to the auto-de-fe chained, shackled and gagged : so the devil can't tempt you to relapse into his perverse doctrines or indulge in the horrendous promiscuity of the most bestial animals

: protecting you against yourselves : so that one day you too can sit at the right hand of the Father, enraptured by the glorious ecstasy of a thousand sublime visions : your soul as snow-white as the lace-edged silk mantillas worn by the young maidens and grand dames watching our fiesta from the box or front row : the smiling face of the Supreme Defender of the Fate of the Fatherland will then look down upon you and no one will be able to cast aspersions on your opinions and doubts, your vile wallowing in animal pleasures : at a stroke your erring ways, despicable acts and wretchedness will be at an end : the Most Pure Virgin will invite you to sup at her table and offer you her most delectable dishes : rather than wasting away in an abject life of vice, eternally bearing that stain, you will temper your spiritual stock at the stake and eliminate the sores malingering in your souls : our Lord has taken pity on your baseness and will rescue you from the dismal darkness you inhabit thanks to this providential crucible of pain and penitence : what an intoxicating comforting prospect! : the auto-de-fe is God's merciful stratagem that enables you to enter through Heaven's gates cleansed and immaculate : like men who have unceasingly led a quiet and virtuous life : shoulder to shoulder, without discrimination, with the standard-bearers of our caste : the burnished impeccable perfect soul of the contrite criminal, of the meek and condemned, is like untreated gold in the sands of the river, nuggets or glinting flakes that, alloyed with copper, are used in the manufacture of jewels, accessories or dentures : but the souls of Moors, Jews, heretics, bigamists or sodomites attain this unblemished exemplary climactic state only after a long and severe process of purgation : you are familiar, I assume, with the gold-bearing pyrites that must be extracted, washed and crushed before they finally yield their noble yellow substance? :

well, that's how the souls of the accused are refined and improved over days, weeks, months or years of sober restrained torture in our dungeons and prisons : and even so, my beloved children, the mineral thus purified remains imperfect : to reach the higher unparalleled ductile state, a series of complex operations requiring the subtle skills of foundry-men and goldsmiths are necessary : we inquisitors must likewise separate the wheat from the chaff, the gold from the magma : the stamina and resignation of those relaxed at an auto do in fact make these residual impurities disappear : with the significant difference that, while melting and purifying gold takes hours and hours, the processing of the soul of those sentenced to the stake is barely a ten-minute thing : what is such a derisory interlude compared to the immortal glory you're being offered! : the lachrymose hypocritical reactions of foreign critics ignore this and omit the all-important factor because the suffering you endure only assumes its real significance when assessed in relation to the fate of your souls : Father, you will say : why must we suffer when you don't? : must we deduce from your words that our arrogant criminal or unclean actions were predestined from ab aeterno? : oh, unfathomable Mystery! : though God knows what's in store, He respects our freedom and, if He tolerates our sinful ways, does so that the chosen may voluntarily set out on the path to redemption : you will have heard of those diamond-bearing lands in the Transvaal where carbon crystallizes into remarkable octahedrons? : in His infinite wisdom, the Lord has arranged things here too so that some crystallizations are transparent and sparkling while others are simply translucent and the vast majority are black as coal : and come the Day of Judgment the Manager of the Mine will classify the three kinds according to their purity and value : the dark souls of the impenitent will be like carbonado used to drill rocks, which all buyers scorn : repentant sinners, the so-called bort, spherical in shape and used by craftsmen to cut precious stones : and those who accept with Christian joy the drastic redeeming sentences handed out by the holiest of tribunals, the precious brilliantly faceted gems we all admire in the display cabinets of jewelers and diamond merchants : saved souls, arctic steppes, eternal Nordically white glaciers! : and does anyone here still want to whinge? : if so, believe me, he deserves all he gets, even the harshest rigors of damnation in hell

SALUS POPULI SUPREMA LEX EST

the results of our vigorous and most practical therapy are there for all to see : governments responsible for the whole world envy our masterly instrument of purification that, by adapting to the customs and needs of each era, century after century, preserves our moral health thanks to the radical elimination of suspected germ carriers and the establishment on our frontiers of an unbreakable sealed cordon sanitaire : today, within the orbit of the civilized Christian world, our country contributes the smallest number of eternal damnations, in both relative and absolute terms : only twenty percent of our compatriots were sentenced last year to endless suffering in hell, a truly derisory number compared to the sum total of reprobates in liberal-democratic, pagan or atheist countries : and we find ourselves equally at the back of the line in the number of blessèd souls in Purgatory as well as in the aggregate of years they'll be expiating there : recent statistics supplied by our computers reveal a remarkable reduction in the number of banned books read, in attendances at insalubrious exhibitions, in cheek-to-cheek canoodling in promiscuous dance-halls, and illicit touching, feeling and stroking : as for manuscripts sent in for the approval of our Department for Orientation and Consulting, we abide by the following criteria : only authorize the publication of works the legitimate Reproductive Little Couple could read aloud without blushing and, in particular, without being aroused, and return everything else stamped with a Not Likely : an arrangement as fair as it is sensible, the righteousness of which not only translates, as might seem at first sight, into a remarkable decline in the number of adulteries but also in the number of indulgences of the flesh other than for the purpose of procreation : nowadays our adolescents don't have recourse, as in other nations, to the ghastly solitary vice and you would need a magnifying glass to catch those guilty of the nefast sin : this hateful crew is so staunchly on the retreat that our glorious national fiesta is under threat! : some provincial authorities have recently raised the alarm and called for a more open-ended policy in order to ensure the ritual staging of autos for decades to come : numerous official parties and tourist groups were dreadfully disappointed last summer when, at the last minute, the masters of ceremonies in several cities had to cancel fiestas to which they'd been invited on the valid pretext of the need to safeguard pride and reputation : the number and pedigree of those condemned failed to meet minimum standards, and offenders were returned to their dungeons amid indignant catcalls from expectant audiences : longstanding and renowned inquisitors and judges from the world of burnings at the stake have sadly been forced to relax foreigners caught in the act or pay in gold guilty parties of much lower quality from other provinces : this imbalance between supply and demand deteriorates daily and, convinced of the virtues of rational planning, our technocrats are embracing a bold policy of prioritizing and austerity to guarantee a normal flow of supplies to tourist areas in future : the debate has spread from elite circles and pressure groups out to the masses and our newspapers print hundreds of readers' letters highlighting the crisis situation and proposing all kinds of options and solutions, harnessing the fauna's proverbially fertile brainwaves that is the envy of other nations : some, for example, favor a staggered incineration of the criminal, namely, the abrupt extinguishing of flames before burns become fatal, thus enabling the individual's speedy recovery in one of our ultra-modern comfortable hospitals so that, after receiving all the love and tender care his wounds require, he can proceed to play the lead role in fiestas in other plazas : others suggest that the dramatic reduction in the number of those relaxed be balanced by a due lengthening of individual punishments, via the use of substances that curb the action of the flames and prolong the life of the condemned for a few minutes : the most foresighted propose the creation of reservations of the sort established by the U.S. of A. for its native Indians, where future reprobates would be permitted bestial sin and barbaric copulation, heretic manuscripts and banned books : others, finally, despairing of the viability of the proposed remedies and certain that active moral preventive measures will banish sin forever from our most hallowed soil, are in favor of establishing a lottery system to assign vacancies at the stake to members of the lowest social orders and to grant the families of those executed compensation higher than the dead-man's wage on top of a plethora of physical and moral benefits equal to those offered to the families of soldiers who have fallen gloriously on the field of battle : advantages of this daring suggestion : it will galvanize the nation's feelings, satisfy the people's centuries-old tastes, maintain the country's prestige abroad and the influx of foreign tourists : our travel agencies and tourist offices could then guarantee the proper staging of the fiesta with a clear conscience, in the same way they can emphatically put their faith in the sun and the cloudless sky, the traditional hospitality of our way of life, the sensual charms of our females, bargain-basement prices and that vague, mysterious je ne sais quoi, the fascination of which is more easily experienced than explained, which constitutes our nation's peculiar difference : disadvantages? : an evident modicum of cruelty and injustice that would expose a weak flank to the embittered resentful pens of our perpetual foes, allowing them to get all hot under the collar at our so-called savagery while they carefully conceal the eloquent flipside of the coin from their readers : the much more cruel and tragic consequences of their renowned policy of tolerance toward the inhabitants of their own countries : the truly terrifying number of souls condemned by their lack of consideration to eternal irreversible punishment : for if the torment at the stake that lasts ten, twenty or forty minutes provokes their sentimental whimpers, how should they react to flames that last not a day, week or year, but an entire, an absolutely entire lifetime? : because hell is much more horrendous and is eternal! : so who then are the real barbarians? : them or us? : who will have shown greater pity, charity and tenderness, the aficionados and habitués at our bonfire nights or that motley crew of human rights defenders, where there isn't a single evangelical pastor, sanctimonious Anglican biddy or mawkish dame who doesn't shed floods of tears over the expiatory essentially benign fates of those we

relax with the fleeting punishment of the stake? : we shall repeat yet
again : a hypocritically humanitarian mindset can never plumb the
depths of the noble purifying virile sentiment that inspires our fiesta : if in the course of the auto it wishes masochistically to identify
with the damned, well, so be it : we, for our part, will simply ask, by
virtue of what rational criterion does it find such an attitude com-
patible with diamantine insensitivity to eternal suffering : or could
it be that torture beyond our borders doesn't move and upset them?
: medice, cura te ipsum! : are you or are you not familiar with the
proverb about the mote in the eye of the other and the beam in your
own? : well, think on it, Mr. Critic, and forget all that drivel!

MONSTRUM HORRENDUM, INFORME, INGENS

our austere and solemn Peninsula has always been a land rich in
heretics, mystics, apostates and eccentrics of every stripe, as well as
male saints and sages, so writes the illustrious Menéndez Pelayo,
and there is certainly something unsettling shady and sin-loving
in the genius of so vibrant a race, whose history, while honored by
a distinguished roll of kings, conquistadors and priests, is sullied
by gangs of individuals who, well off the beaten track, have tried to
sustain the secret worship of reptiles and other lascivious animals
from bygone times, reneging on God, his law, his saints and embracing the devil as their lord and master, sometimes in the shape
of a hirsute simian, sometimes in the likeness of a handsome Moor,
celebrating vile witches' sabbaths wherein they revere him with
kisses and genuflections as preliminaries to strange wild festivities
wherein they perform all manner of bestial coupling and sordid

acts, which we shan't tarry to describe for aesthetic reasons or as a matter of good taste : crimes narrated in scrupulous detail by the sinners themselves and corroborated by numerous witnesses called in front of our righteous and infallible courts, like that recently burnt truculent evildoer who insolently defended his execrable devotion to the serpent and went on to confess that male ob strepitus audiebat nocturnes, prima nocte incubum sensisse, sed cum olives negras coena comedisset, naturale existimasse, even anticipating in his morbid ravings the coming of a huge monstrous gorilla whose might would spread to the ends of the earth, a fateful prophecy and ominous augury that, though articulated in a dry monotone, terrified the members of that learned auspicious assembly, forcing them to draw astrological lines and have recourse to wizards and excommunicators who, in an awesome spectacular pronouncement that served to gather the whole nation around the miraculous image of the Virgin, solemnly proceeded to excommunicate the ophidians, forcing them through vehement imprecations and effective spells to take flight in a hurry, a black cloud eclipsing the sun as they moved in droves towards the coasts of Africa whence they had come in an evil hour, perhaps searching for that fantastic avenging simian whom the man at the stake, in the throes of his death agony, had begged in vain for release, blasphemously invoking him by the absurd barbaric name of King Kong

HOC VOLO, SIC JUBEO, SIT PRO RATIONE VOLUNTAS

so that any faint glimmer of the idea that sovereignty resides outside my royal personage is erased from our soil, so my people know that I will never contemplate the slightest change in the fundamental laws of the Monarchy, and, considering the various customs and practices condoned by their long use and adaptation over the centuries, I have ordered a Council of Sages be created of men of authority, representatives of the domestic hearth and other fine upstanding citizens, empowered to enumerate to my beloved subjects all the authoritative arguments that give sustenance to the providential divine power incarnate in my august and lordly will, bidding them to inform the people of a tiny number of elementary notions that can be accessed by even the dimmest and simplest of folk, in order to counter the underhand dissemination of doctrines from elsewhere according to which citizens should be responsible before the law and should decide the future of the nation following a sinister mathematics of the majority, summarily discounting the huge mass of historical evidence accumulated over centuries of governance by our revered dynasty and forthwith to focus attention on the philosophical heart of the matter : the scientific basis of our benevolent though undeniable superiority : manifested not only in the distinctly peculiar circumstances surrounding our eminently poetic propagation, thanks to a delicate convoluted process that, a thousand leagues from viviparous plebeian placenta-based reproduction, engages in a splendid sequence of blossoming, pollinating and fertilizing, sometimes like flowers with neither chalice nor corolla, being pollinated by the gentle discreet blowing of the breeze, sometimes like gaudy blooms oozing scented nectar and attracting specimens of the most motley species of winged insect but also, and quintessentially, in a most exquisite ultra-refined digestive system that excludes, from the onset, any dropping of putrid visceral matter or abject evacuation of individual sewers : or do those mendacious little upstarts rashly spreading their abstruse and peculiar theories perhaps think that my royal person and the members of my revered family defecate in honking ditches and wash their bore-holes with a tin of water? : the idea would be a hoot if it weren't so sacrilegious, and those who defend such a whopper could never substantiate it because as simple natural reason indicates if solid or liquid visceral emissions and other bodily emanations like hair, sweat, nails, saliva and mucous matter existed, they would partake of my august self's sovereign nature and would thus have been lovingly preserved by my most faithful and intimate subjects and servants as emblems or signs of my invincible power : but as we find no mention of such treasures in the annals of History, we must conclude, consensus omnium, nemine discrepante, that they never existed, and that my exalted person and the members of my family are not party to the same animal necessities that afflict the hoi polloi, obliging them to restore to the earth, in such a filthy and disgusting form, what they received from it in the guise of delicious tidbits and mild refreshing cordials : it is precisely here that the egalitarian hypothesis collapses and reveals itself as truly ridiculous : it is no secret that animals and humans are patently inferior to plants and trees : the latter's superfluities are delightful and lovely, while those of bipeds and quadrupeds nauseate and disgust : and if we find the former pleasing and are attracted by the aroma and taste of their fruits, who but the devil could relish the filthy horrible offerings from human and animal entrails? : here lies the rub! : who would dare argue that my distinguished enlightened self is qualitatively inferior to mere vegetable species? : any suckling babe would indignantly reject such a nonsense! : naturally, some arrogant democrat, acting the smart-ass, will risk the question : don't

Their Most Gracious Majesties eat? : newspapers, magazines and TV bulletins report quite the contrary : so, do tell us : what happens to the tidbits his regal person consumes if he doesn't excrete them? : oh, pettifogging know-alls, that's what I was coming to! : if the metabolism of the vegetable kingdom differs from those of animals and humans, what's so strange or surprising if your just and most exalted sovereign's is different too? : while plebeian and republican nefast eyes secrete putrefaction and impurities, those belonging to your ancient dynasty exude sweet fragrances : our Lord, in His infinite wisdom, has ordained that creatures on earth rise above the animal state and its rotten secretions at a rate relative to their merits until they attain the ideal of the saints and the blessèd in Paradise whose residues, St. Bernard tells us, are transformed into a sweet and pleasant liquid, similar to frankincense and essence of myrrh : God, through His Divine Mediatrix, gradually raises his creatures to the highest level of fragrance, and rewarding services given by our devout and holy family, He has allowed it to clamber one step further up the steep stairs leading from stench to scent, from quadruped to angel and has shown as much to the world via a simple and edifying miracle : the act of giving off, without sound or fury, in a noble restrained manner, the most varied array of aromas, essences and balsams that, artistically packaged in little flasks and phials designed by our best artists, can be purchased in the country's main pharmacies and drugstores at a price all our competitors will find impossible to beat : their inimitable exemplary qualities have immediately earned them the public's favor and finally seen off traditional market domination by French products that are as affected as they are inorganic, driving them from our burgeoning market with half a dozen deservedly prestigious names

: "Breath of a Royal," "Dynastic Magic," "Princely Smile," "Nuits dans les jardins du palais," "Baiser suzerain," "Fleur monarchique," and there isn't a single posh lady or fashionable gent who doesn't buy and use them, delighted to waft around a fragrant aura that is at once a seal of personal distinction and a masterly synthesis of the grandeur and magnificence of our Monarchy

NATURA NON FACIT SALTUS

such a fine outstanding notion gradually permeated the class system, giving rise to a noble rivalry among their members with respect to the position they occupy on the odorous ladder : classification by levels or layers assumes the characteristics of a unique theogony, dirty squatting plebs at the bottom and His Sublime Wingèd Majesty at the top : between the two extremes, this extraordinarily strict scale of values replaces and much to our advantage, the economically driven and thus precarious social stratification prevailing in other countries : instead of the you-are-worth-what-you-own of deplorably materialist countries we have established a give-me-a-sniff-and-I'll-tell-you-who-you-are that's become the official norm in our immutable caste system : everyone has his or her place, according to scent or stench, obeying the sage prescient dispensations of He in the wings, the director who is staging the solemn passion play that climaxes in the Great Theater of the World : sparing us the din, turmoil and turbulence of History's stormy seas, bringing tumult and revolution, uprisings and struggles in their wake and awareness that life is a dream and all is fickle, changing and ephemeral when compared to the stark reality of death : some perch daintily on the bowl of an elegant secluded toilet, others crouch over a hole in the ground, and then the worst off, habitués of that stinking putrid trench into which they shoot their dung, detritus and diarrhea, take pleasure in filthy defecation and even yield without shame or blushing cheeks to the execrable vice of sodomy : a criminal barbaric act, once the preserve of dark and degenerate races, that has always extended its tentacles into our midst, possibly in response to a celestial strategy to ensure that the autos-de-fe can continue, and its utility, nonexistent at first sight, thus seems justified : at present, the individuals occupying the ladder's higher rungs have successfully slimmed down the volume and shape of their rears through an arduous process of purging, transforming them into superfluous ornamental organs that distinguish them from those whose rude insulting curves parade their vile parentage with base matter : armed with their new squeaky-clean dignity, these subjects can now concentrate quietly on fruitful study and meditation, the envy of foreign university professors and scientists : rather than the usual round of mathematics, physics, anatomy, natural history, etcetera, the eternal repetition of which becomes monotonous even for the most ordinary small-minded citizen, our great brains prefer to plumb bottomless wells of casuistry or the fascinating world of ethereal syllogisms : for example the debates raging in lecture halls over the make up of the heavens : are they made of bell-metal or are they liquid, like the most invigorating wine? : two eminent theologians polemicize in our newspapers as to whether angels can or cannot transport human beings through the air from Lisbon to Madrid : and, recently, a pioneer of flights through space, after keeping to a strictly birdlike diet and calculating the exact ratio of four ounces of feathers to carry two pounds of flesh, glued the corresponding amount of the latter to different parts of his body, manufactured two wings he then tied to his arms, and, feathered thus, cast himself to the winds from the tower of Plasencia Cathedral, whizzing into the clouds, according to his disciples or screwing up in the act according to his rivals, at any rate pioneering the path to recent advances in structural and generative angelology, a branch of learning wherein, as in the study of the Paraclete and its properties, we have established what can be considered a firm pre-eminence over the learned scholars of other nations, hence consolidating the fatherland's unique position in the universal history of science

VIDEO MELIORA PROBOQUE, DETERIORA SEQUOR

and thus, the Creator, situating man, who is of His making, in the world, namely, between heaven and hell, in terms of abode, between eternity and time, in terms of length of life, between Himself and the devil in terms of freedom and between angels and animals, in terms of nature, He has turned him, one could say, into the fulcrum of Creation, a point of necessary convergence for the greatest mesh of internal relationships via which he is linked to all things and all things are linked to him in a complex subtle architecture where each tiny pebble, brick or element, however apparently insignificant, nonetheless performs a vital role, so much so that if it disappeared it would prompt the total collapse of the entire spectacular edifice, a perfect product, we do declare, of the unknowable will of Our Lord : and one factor, at first sight petty and contemptible, is no doubt the powerful inclination to return to the earth, in a sad pitiful squat, the food and fruits received thereof in the form of pleasant tasty tidbits, obeying a divine plan carefully designed to underline our dual or intermediary status, midway between sublime heavenly creatures and vicious brutish animals, a most mean contemptible inclination, but one it is in our power to control and defeat if we take our inspiration from countless sages, exalted monarchs and illustrious dictators, those the Great and Merciful One has granted great prerogatives, stipulating they should be revered and honored and making them the cat's whiskers whilst everyone else is but the dregs in the sieve and thus we struggle heroically and tenaciously, never surrendering to the lethal despondency that frequently comes after a fall, raising ourselves up again and again, stout of spirit and unflinchingly trusting in Our Lord : Father, some will say : the resistance you recommend is beyond us : we have tried not once, but hundreds, nay, thousands of times, and have always relapsed into evil ways : in vain have we led healthy well-ordered lives, guarding against opportunities to sin abominably on every path leading to the latrine : in vain have we driven scatological thoughts from our minds and closed our eyes and ears to those wallowing in the grossest coarsest bestiality : temptation assails us night and day, our entrails seem to dilate, our senses attack us vigorously, our intellects begin to mist over and shameful frailty possesses our bodies, unleashing a series of reflexes that drive us almost blindly towards the public trench, urging us to squat like savages and finally capitulate with a relief and satisfaction that puts us into melt down and stuns us, stripping us of right reason for minutes on end, after which we wake up sad and sorrowful, souls contrite and hearts broken, beating our breasts and desperate for forgiveness : this is the sad reality, Father : we want to fly, be free as angels, yet we crash-land, badly : the devil tweaks our nefast eye, forces us to crouch and, using his perverse arts to broaden the black sewer we ignominiously offer him, he triumphantly contemplates our pathetic spasm, rejoices in our fall and the feebleness of fragile human wills, subjecting us to his dread tyranny, taking us away from God's love : I know all this only too well and would simply tell anyone who came to cry on my shoulder after a new and shocking relapse : my child, never give up all hope : quantumvis multa atque enormia fuerint peccata tua, nunquam de venia desperabis : corruisti? : surge, converte te ad Medicum animae tuae : et viscera pietatis ejus tibi patebunt : iterum corruisti? : iterum surge, geme, clama, et miseratio Redemptoris tui te suscipiet : corruisti tertio, et quarto, et saepius? : surge rursum, plange, suspira, humiliate : Deus tuus non te deseret : and one of these days, unexpectedly, the miracle will happen : you will stop shitting! : suddenly your tension, anguish, tightness and cramps will disappear : a physiological and psychic calm, a corporeal and spiritual serenity will gradually suffuse your soul, raising you from the sad wretched mass to that delightful abode which only the chosen inhabit : your waste will then be eliminated through your skin and will be fragrant and charming : surrounded by kings, warriors and saints you will live eternally in a sweet-smelling paradise of harmony and peace

ETIAMSI OMNES, EGO NON

a genuinely moving example of heroic perseverance in pursuit of goodness, because of the strange circumstances and very tender age of the protagonist, is of course the blessèd child Alva-rito whose process of sanctification in the Roman Curia already has the backing of eminent theologians and the active support of thousands upon thousands of devout religious and pious souls : born into the heart of an illustrious patrician family which had made an honest fortune in the Pearl of the Caribbean where it is famed for its apostolic zeal and philanthropic spirit, the budding saint received the punctilious Christian education befitting offspring of his stock, displaying from the earliest age a remarkably profound devotion to the Mysteries of our revealed religion and in particular to the Immaculate Conception of the Virgin : rather than running to join in the cheerful innocent games of childhood with the rest of his schoolmates, he preferred to withdraw to the private family oratory and, kneeling at the altar, far from bustling streets and madding crowds, he would spend hours on end absorbed in grave and abstruse meditation : his intense awareness of the putrid nature of the human body and its powerful inclination to animal outpourings and impure secretions made him toss and turn in his sleep : mentally he contrasted the melancholy reality of discharge from the bowels with the beautiful ideal of the saints and blessèd in Paradise, whose residues, St. Bernard tells us, are converted into a refined soothing liquid, like balsam of frankincense and essence of myrrh : the daily act of defecating into the lovely enameled porcelain chamber pot, fashioned by a renowned craftsman, filled him with anguish and gloom : the cheery eye, painted at the bottom, with the motto I CAN SEE YOU, made him feel that the seepage from his entrails into that dark loathsome sewer coveted by the devil was an irremediable disaster : in his heart of hearts he couldn't resist evoking that other Eye that in his governess's pious tracts symbolized God's almighty presence and the idea that he might be a sacrilegious profaner depressed him to such a degree his abdomen instinctively contracted and his fecal matter failed to push its way out : his condition deteriorated by the day to such an extent that his parents, fearing for his health, try every means to cure him : the most famous doctors, consulted in the emergency, prescribe powerful laxatives : the quantity and violence of his temptations increases, but our saint gladly submits to the tests and hurdles that make his enterprise all the more difficult and steels his will : ensconced on the potty, linen vest lifted slightly and velvet breeches folded back to the knee, motionless, he resists his body's base defeatist inclinations for hours on end, silently imploring God and his Heavenly Mother for help : wet-nurses and maids take turns at his side with purgatives and medications, straining to detect on his impassively angelic face the much-trumpeted impact of the inevitable glycerine suppository: in vain do they force him to stand up so they can eagerly inspect the results : time and again they will only discover the vigilant unpolluted eye of the pot : nothing, nothing yet! : Alvarito sits down again, decorous and dignified, with a sober and mature expression that astounds even those who only know him by sight, never betrays for a second a trace of his inner turmoil, the savage battle being waged by his contradictory impulses : he boldly scorns the advice from the wily serpent in a magnificent tableau his biographers paint in profuse detail that we will extensively reproduce here, given that the scene is so intensely dramatic and paradigmatic : on the right, God, the Most Holy Virgin, and their retinue of servants and archangels : on the left, a band of malign serpents gathered around the horrid monstrous gorilla that has come from Africa : in the middle, ensconced on his enameled porcelain potty, a fair-haired dimple-cheeked child sur-

veys the verbal jousting of these irreconcilable antagonists under
the weightless subtle protection of a resplendent halo, as broad as
Saturn's ring, miraculously suspended over his graceful head

SERPENT : why keep resisting your instincts? : can't you see you're
   torturing yourself to no avail? : if you take heed of my advice,
   you'll enjoy immediate relief and be incredibly happy

GUARDIAN ANGEL : the pleasure he promises only lasts a few seconds! : think of your soul! : of the grief you will cause the Virgin!

SERPENT : relax those muscles! : loosen that intestine! : give in! :
   see how easy it is!

GUARDIAN ANGEL : no, no, Alvarito, ignore him!

SERPENT : stop your suffering! : stop constraining your rear passage!

GUARDIAN ANGEL : no, no, he's tricking you!

SERPENT : do as I say! : give in to your impulses! : satisfy your body!
   : just see how you'll die of pleasure!!

ANGELIC CHOIR : no, Alvarito, no!

and our future saint, with that powerful self-control that comes
from such serene unblemished faith, contracts his sphincters and
completely blocks his hole, invoking fervently the help promised
by the Lord : meanwhile, the Master Up There swings in his hammock, in a suit and panama just like Great-grandfather's and the
Virgin, nervously, dead scared, frantically watches out for the end-
result through her opera glasses

Marita, my daughter, can you hear me?

yes, Papa

what is that lovely little boy up to, the nice offspring of the owners
of the Cruces sugar-mill?

he's still sitting on his potty

still resisting?

he'd rather be dead than excrete!

pleased to hear it! : long may he persevere! : what about his doctors?

they've inserted yet another suppository

poor kid! : do you figure he'll last out?

he has a will of iron

will alone is not enough : tell him to pray to Me!

he's already praying

do you know if he's recited petitions to the Most Holy Trinity?

yes, I think so

well, ask him to repeat them : that's the advice from my best theologians

all right, Papa

the Trisagion will help him hold on : oh, and if temptation gets too strong, strap a scapular round his neck!

I've got a very good one right here

off you go then, see him and tell him he is in my thoughts and I keep blessing him

the Girl is preparing to descend with two lovely bits of spun cloth tied with ribbons when a single tender-loving miracle crowns Alvaro's superhuman efforts : evacuation without sound or fury, in noble sweet-smelling mode! : emotions run high and blissful tears glisten in the eyes of the numerous spectators : King Kong and his serpents beat an immediate retreat and the heavenly hierarchies and choirs intone their prayers and antiphons amid sweet arpeggios and the fluttering of wings

what's happening? asks Great-grandfather : why are my angels so excited?

they're singing victory anthems!

what's the victory?

he's won! : Papa, he's won!

who? : the boy?

yes, Papa, I swear to it!

child, how happy you've made me!

he's just exuded a fragrant substance through his skin!

does it smell sweet?

better than French perfume!

catch it in a jar : that'll be a real relic someday!

I'll put it in my own atomizer

you like it that much?

the scent's a knock-out!

bring the chamber pot a bit nearer!

yes, try it

you're absolutely right!

ah, quelle volupté divine!

what was that, child?

it's sublime, Papa : like, like a poem by Lamartine : enough to make
one believe in God!

AD AUGUSTA PER ANGUSTA

the nasal whine is irritating and you stop your transcription,
with the no-less-abrupt-for-being-premeditated determination of
someone who, defending himself against assault by radio, violently
silences the airwaves by furiously pressing a button : you return
afresh to the host of testimonies crammed into your tiny library and
the drawers of your ramshackle filing cabinet : in that attic room

where you stubbornly surrender to the expert onanism of writing : the age-old nonproductive act of grasping the pen and allowing its generative flow of secretions to spurt to the beat of your will : from the masterpiece of that astute Archpriest of Talavera who, apparently subject to the servitude of moral discourse, managed to discover on the sly the hidden genius of a language that nowadays lies rather fallow after a hundred years of exhaustion in what was an abnormally fertile century, what with texts by thick-skinned provosts and bold iconoclasts, even in a homemade Havana publication that x-rays and strips bare your sugarocrat family's history of oppression : lingering in particular on those authors whose acute awareness of the nation's ills caused them to agonize over the country's decrepit state and the possible remedies : conscientiously setting out diagnoses and suitable medicines, prescriptions and formulae : looking inwards or outwards, modernity or self-absorption : panaceas recommended not once but dozens of times, in different tones and registers, never getting it clear (like you now) that neither the enlightened and prolific Benedictine, nor the worthy prisoner in Bellver, nor the melancholy self-banished Spaniard, nor the lucid suicidal visionary, nor the renowned generation of the Salamanca owl, nor those who came (and are still coming) in their footsteps succeeded in discovering the real root of our catastrophes : the image of the fair-haired angelic infant royally poised on his potty may perhaps point you in the right direction and inspire a solution in the process : a centuries-long constipated country (his), also lolling on a throne of self-sufficiency whose satin cushion hides from the public eye the secret of a circular cavity, where, sheltered by the sides of the settle, the sublime sublimating device lurks, waiting, respectfully though impatiently, on the now superannuated

112

chamber pot that historically precedes this beloved child of puritan prurience, the last fling of the mighty English industrial revolution of yesteryear : while a band of arrogant quacks and officious physicians pursue the patient in vain with suppositories, laxatives and purges : the real state of the nation, should be represented, not as is usual, by the hieratic figure of the austere conqueror of *The Surrender of Breda* or the very upright *Knight with a Hand on his Chest*, but in the shape of a lean solemn silent hidalgo, also straight out of a canvas by Velázquez or El Greco, but legs tucked in, leaning slightly forward, so that the fine pleated material of his breeches hides the round edge of the receptacle theoretically destined to receive a solid donation, indifferent to pleas and requests, siren songs and worldly pressures, lauded by panegyrists for his exemplary patience and Christian resilience and, all in all tight, greedy, miserly and deaf to the exhortations of doctors who with enemas, laxatives and syrup of figs try in vain to loosen his sluice and facilitate the delayed delivery while, august and unperturbed like Philip the Second, he greets their frantic gestures and dire concerns with a cavernous cursory "hush" : the country's century-old rectal constriction, hard-won measly offerings would thus not be the consequence of any innate predisposition to metaphysics (as the orthodox platypus asserts) or of a ruthless repressive diet (as its victims maintain), but rather (as you now concur) the result of a persistent quirk of the digestive system, transmuted by flawed diagnosis and lack of proper treatment, into an incurably chronic disease : which would in the end explain the paucity of its shriveled stools (particularly when compared to those of ancient rivals) : the stodgy stolid soporific and lumpy works that have always characterized its literary-scientific output and (indeed, why not) the miraculous secretion of dense sweet-smelling pearls that no nose (human or divine) could inhale without feeling intense delight and a genuine groveling admiration : a country (his) where gradually endemic lethal creeping aches, pains and disorders have entered an actively contagious stage and their subsequent paroxysms, virulence and persistence are expressed in a wealth of symptoms that in turn augur fresh complications and aggravating factors that banish all hope of relief or alleviating operations in clinics, hospitals or medical centers : a seemingly fatal process, beyond cure or therapy, that makes celebrated specialists speak in terms of the end of the road, even though the solution is at hand (forget learned treatises), in best-selling medical manuals and encyclopedias : just consult (as you do) the chapter referring to the paucity or infrequency of stools and (internal or external) causes : irregular eating habits, poor intake of liquids, weak intestinal muscles, lack of peristaltic activity : and proceed to implement various measures that are quite self-evident : circuit-training, massaging of the abdomen, open-air exercises before or after meals, hot or cold showers in the lumbar region : not forgetting the tried and tested diet of (raw or cooked) vegetables, fruit (above all plums and grapes), a hundred and fifty grams of honey, a glass of cold water or milk drunk on an empty stomach : oh, and most of all, immediately stop using the potty or water-closet in favor of time-honored, now much-scorned bowel-emptying methods! : incorrect positioning during the process can constitute a serious obstacle to an opportune liberation of the intestine : rather than settling down on a horizontal seat sixteen inches above the ground (or rather less than half that in the case of a chamber pot) the constipated individual (or country) should squat, preferably leaning their feet on a raised step, ten inches above the ground : such a posture (we guarantee!) encourages the proper working of the abdominal muscles that instigates movement around the bends and represents a weighty argument on the lips of those who advocate optimal relaxation of the rear passage and a return to the old delightful pleasures of plopping in the public trench

V

I

you will leap into the future tense : prescription, compulsion, certainty? : at any rate a subjective mode : without the third-person endorsement in the indefinite past tense appropriate for historic declarations and their glossy veneer of truth : with a mere squiggle of the pen joining that tiny but smiling pleiad of utopian ethereal dreamers who ever since the denigrated Century of Lights have been trying to salvage the dour country of your ancestors from its arrogant natural lack of reason? : distinguished encyclopedists, members of enlightened corporations, proponents of progress in field and factory, virtuous citizens useful to the fatherland who, according to your perennial high priest of orthodoxy, believed with pigeon-brained naïveté, that merely by giving out farmland deeds and founding economic enterprises they would seed, as if by magic, artificial meadows, cotton manufacturing and trading companies, changing deserts and untilled land into gardens of Eden where abundance and prosperity would reign unchecked : idyllic daydreams, bucolic visions, which, extending into every branch of social life, would allow fantasy to spin subtle strategies for education and communal life following models from Greek and Roman antiquity, altogether alien to the huge hostile mass ignorant and brutish like few others but adept nonetheless in deriding the fruits of these homegrown philanthropic humanists : rural aristocrats, shepherd kings, clever inventors of abstruse pneumatic machinery immortalized in watercolors and on canvas against the blissful honest backdrop of a pleasant Swiss landscape! : a utopia as quickly destroyed as it was rebuilt in the course of the bourgeois industrial revolution, while in stony surly climes the scenes of violence captured or hallucinated by the great deaf painter unraveled apace in the sinister glow of gunpowder and smoke, the prelude to fresh, now inextinguishable fires : a gloomy sequence of events that, belying all possible expectations, perhaps sparked off one of the outbreaks of boils that was to plague the most lucid spirit of the time : the author, as is well-known, of strictly scientific analyses that, though set against frivolous fantasizing, would nonetheless give rise, quite paradoxically, to those grandiose social edifices history offers us as a model, where captains of opposing stripe hoist the sayings of the "London Moor" with reckless youthful enthusiasm : humani nihil a me alienum puto : o rational creature, perfectible being, dearly beloved New Man, brain stripped of base needs and instincts, simple sociable and good-hearted, advancing rapidly down the straight and narrow paths of order, progress and happiness! : when society and the individual are no longer terms in conflict and harmful individualism melds into one unanimous majestic social arpeggio : chaste salubrious Valkyries toiling next to tractors : ear of wheat turning to song, song to ear of wheat : heavy swell of golden corn rippling in the wind as if undulating to the sounds of a victorious military march! : happily married brilliant hydroelectric-engineer or wife responsible for an ultra-modern petrochemical complex and husband furrowing through vast constellated outer space, portrayed with their numerous staggered permanently smiling offspring : children and yet more bug-eyed children dazzled by a splendiferous future, par l'avenir lumineux of a vital project sans bavures, that in turn guarantees an existence free of anxiety and stress, where the vices and sores of the previous degenerate society will never take hold : nobody will exploit anyone : love will be the equivalent of a freely entered contract : man will be peaceful harmonious and honest : the previous division between face and ass will be suppressed, the entire process of sublimation! : individuals without destructive urges, subject to no physiological laws, no spasms from violent erections! : a paradise that proscribes duality and rejects dichotomy, snatches the bestial slave crouching over the trench and hurls him up to sublimely perfect, saccharinely white heights : bodies that neither enjoy nor are enjoyed, deprived of that blackest hole and its vile uses : pastel-toned postcards of present-day assless utopias : interminable tide of faces that laugh, sing, listen to and recite works by the Chief, but don't fuck or shit, don't get stiffies or stools : blind in the lower most useful eye : stripped of the radically generic common denominator that makes men equal and abolishes false hierarchies : fibbing fallacious Eden, whose proper functioning necessarily involves those shamefaced eyes deep in the gruyère, where, as in the cellars and kitchens of the bourgeoisie, the repressed returns, explodes and the banished ass takes its revenge : asylums, cells, torture, engines of an obscene pulsing and splattering that generously hits the trench's mephitic expanse full on amid their feverish straining and panting : defecation, sodomy, filth, attributes of the tortuous sewer that permit and foment sage reconciliation : undivided homo sapiens at home in his dung, detritus and diarrhea : face and ass on a level, free and out in the open, utopia of a complex world, without asepsis or subterfuge : world where the rude insulting curve, flaunting its connections with filthy matter, stretches from the slave holding to the plantation's top management : paradise, yours, a cock and butt story, where metaphor-language subjects object to verb and, released from their chains and dungeons, words, treacherous elusive words, at last quiver dance copulate strip off and flesh out

II

with no guide or comrade minder you will move into the Square of the Revolution (physical physiological anatomical functional circulatory respiratory etcetera, as conceived by that brilliant visionary Rodez), through the thick motley human carpet covering the whole of the sugar-mill yard (an image reproduced dozens of times by the innocuous camera of the paparazzo) and get close (as if you were his double) to the platform that reflects the fortune of the lucky freedmen of today

take a good look : their faces will seem very familiar : announcements on radio, television and in the press have gathered them opposite the rough and ready dais and the hustling blasts from the loudspeakers summon the stragglers who've traveled from recreation and copulation centers on the outskirts to a special live viewing of this portentous happening : the tropical sun blisters down on their heads and they protect themselves as best they can, with colored handkerchiefs and rustic palm-frond hats : mingling with them, the females fan themselves, gesturing femininely, flirtatious as ever despite the dust, dirt and their now threadbare leisure wear : comrade stewards channel the people towards the last few empty spaces and volunteers of both sexes carefully check out the podium on the platform, draped in carpets and hangings where, more than likely, when the time is ripe, the collective leadership will put in an appearance

you break off for a few seconds to sketch in the details : sofas, rocking chairs, hammocks, a grand piano for the musical little girl, bowls of ferns, baskets of fruit, bouquets of flowers? : the oval portrait of a domineering great-grandmother, a servile mulatto boy fending the flies off with a yarey palm frond? : descriptions of customs of the era of Cecilia Valdés which introduce on cue the brassy notes of a catchy burlesque march : while the director's thoughtful moves will focus the attention of the worthy public on the line of vacant thrones that, erected on the damascened dais and protected from the sun by an airy canopy, are clearly waiting for the sovereign presence that, like the pyx amid the gold of the monstrance, will immediately grant them their raison d'être, its magical resplendence filling them to the brim with august power : a liturgical symbol the mere existence of which stuns and fulminates, subdues and enslaves : endowed perhaps with satin cushions whose lovely embroidered hems conceal from the dismal rabble the secrets of a multiple circular cavity, beneath which, sheltered by the sides of the settle, they look out, waiting respectfully, impatiently, on the sublimating devices, the last swan-sodding-song of the English industrial revolution? : no chance! : now expressly so to enable its virtual occupants to survey through the portholes open in the backs, symmetrically level as in a transatlantic liner's cabins, the exultant mass of the citizenry at the apogee and glory of their victorious inalienable freedom : fraternal society without ranks or hierarchies, unified forever thanks to its members' conscious pos-

120

session of that common nether face, whose single gimlet eye scornfully contemplates the grotesque derisory efforts of anyone who stupidly insists on sticking out, being top dog and giving orders : spirited hymns, ballads, songs blare out from the loudspeakers to calm the restless crowd or perhaps prepare the way for the luscious biconvex apparition : the simultaneous surge of a dozen or so faces of the humble executive committee basking in the anonymity of their exemplary perfect equality : not pilots, captains or guides : a yard apart following sensible stage rules, duly squatting down and offering the cheerful assembly, through the holes in the back flaps, those jovial round-faced parts that some naturist photographers at the turn of the century liked to capture, for the delectation of those so inclined, in the act of rivaling, in happy unison, Aeolus's ruddy cheeks : artfully playing their varied panoply of wind instruments : flutes, fifes and flageolets, oboes, clarinets and saxophones : obeying the baton of the snapshot's invisible author, who, like you, is gazing ecstatically at the butt, behind, cheeks, hindquarters, miraculously imbued with supreme executive power : also futilely trying to associate rumps and asses with the letters of the Latin alphabet that sibyllinely identify the unnamed members of the leadership : face A generalísimo secretary-general climaxing his poetic efforts, a murky half-moon B softly sibilant, a smug palmetto C screwed into a funny scowl : as in fairground booths where the artist leaves empty spaces corresponding to the heads of the figures painted on the curtain so eventual customers can be photographed wearing the garb of a clown, sailor or boxer, these entirely interchangeable faces seem to proclaim the undeniable truth of merely temporary functions, essentially unstable, replaceable and unrestrictedly open to every individual in society : posts that are not for life or by right, repressive or perpetual, but ephemeral and subject to going out of date on the basis of the leveling equality of their most commonplace eyes : a picture postcard that, in all its lyrical effusiveness, only half captures the political range of the scene you are meticulously trying to depict : the jubilant delectable succession of round full-cheeked faces contemplating you and the elated mass, as if they wanted to snap you and laugh at you the same way you laugh at them, with the sudden nervousness of someone splitting their sides and releasing long-repressed tension via a short-sharp evacuation : the ribaldry is mutual and, after the enlightening demonstration is over, the jocund donors, having plopped, proceed to eliminate the traces of their sudden euphoria with the minimal movement of a hand wiping away the remains of a smile : sinking it immediately into the nearby pitcher under the approving gaze of those spectators who in the necessary pause for ablutions will have simply and spontaneously taken possession of the stage : Great-grandfather Agustín and his wife, the young master, the girls, a group of poor but worthy relatives, the household slaves, a twittering band of wet-nurses? : the people, sovereign at last, owner and artificer of its own destiny, whose playful African instincts contrast the delights of idle leisure with the age-old shackles of slavery : face after uniform identical face, analogous to those who at the end of the encounter make a disciplined exit through their thrones' circular openings and take up once again without undue ceremony the duties and burdens of their roles : obscure, ignored and anonymous : willingly subjecting themselves to the humble act of squatting, to the good-natured bain de foule that unites them with the flow of the crowd : oh happy niggers leaving the vast yard of the sugar-mill on their way to the leisure centers while the resident lunatic reasoner announces in your ear-hole the program of the genuine subversive Revolution

III

one of most noteworthy idiosyncrasies of our system (if the set of open-ended exceptions addressed can be described as such, deftly avoiding, as it does, any principle or norm) is the peculiar way we fight dictators and the sordid gross aftermaths of the stolid cult of personality : rather than shy away from the problem by condemning, say, the posters, statues and photographs that in other countries usually replicate the determined-inspired, rodin-esquepensive faces of the chief and his team of valiant helmsmen, we have opted to multiply the active signs of their presence but restricting them to the hidden parts of the body that a deeply rooted ancestral prejudice has taught us to scorn, despite their noble physiological function : we contrast the elitism, authoritarianism and hierarchy inherent in the two-eyed, in-yer-face face and the plebeian, bog-standard genius of its symmetrical nether coin : that other cleft lunar face whose penetrating polyphemic eye presides over digestive and reproductive joys with lip-lickin' simplicity, often combined with acts of exuberantly gratuitous pleasure : no quibbling about budgets, over-spending or profitability : installing its image expressly in state offices and bars, bedrooms and leisure centers, public monuments and avenues : huge full-color portraits designed to suggest to today's fortunate citizens the democratic and popular nature of our improvised collective leadership : the lowest common denominator negating superiority in features,

grouping the mass of freedmen around its firm unitary emblem :
preferably snapped at that grandiose moment when offering up the
poetic first fruits of spring, cheeks gripped tight in the effort, a severe and distinguished physiognomy radiating an at once humble
and masterful dignity : or whistling an hilariously catchy gently
modulated melody, prologue to the jovial irrepressible explosion :
a delightful shot similarly popularized on postage stamps issued by
our carefree republic and lovingly hoarded by philatelists fond of
the rare and the odd : not forgetting, while we're about it, the prints
and playing cards, medals, bank notes, gadgets, record covers : an
ubiquitous profusion of anonymous bare-cheeked headless faces,
the random matching of which lies at the heart of an original lottery and betting system via which our indolent citizenry gets rich
quick without a stroke of honest toil : merely by establishing the
link between the beatific mug on display and the letter of the alphabet representing the select member of the leadership : the winner
gets loads of cash and, if he has the right physical features for the
job, will in turn be promoted to the ephemeral dignity of leader
and the exercise of the grandeur and servitude of public service
from the bowel

IV

yet another peculiarity : no national flag or anthem : radical categorical opposition to all institutionalizing, mummifying and
masking : behavior in line with the idea that man is mutable and
doesn't fit any formal paradigm unless we previously extirpate his
ability to change and prosper : we consequently advise all our dip-

lomats and delegations abroad invited to international congresses or sporting events : reject all deceptive identification with banners, pavilions and anthems : abandon your ridiculous role as spokesmen : define yourselves in the negative : but, if the audience in the hall or stadium insists on and demands an emblem on the flagpole corresponding to our anonymous republic, don't hold back : give them satisfaction : choose some rag or other (underpants stained by semen and skid-marks, nylon knickers of a prepubescent lass, the ancient jammy roll of a disgusting sanitary towel) and solemnly hoist it up the pole to a blaring upbeat tune, a gay burlesque : short list of candidates : *Madelon*, the march from *The Bridge on the River Kwai*, "Come Together" by the Beatles, "Fever" in La Lupe's hurricane version : and mustn't forget! : "El congo" or "Mi coquito," by the tasty rumbera whose voraciously pagan mouth is all smiles on that shiny LP sleeve, wouldn't be a bad idea either

V

get used to your own base matter : put behind you any neurotic hysterical relationship with your nether facial duo and its cute tender offspring : death to the concealment procedure as hatched by pathetic puritanical capital and its absurd noxious after-effects : retention, accumulation, constipation in league with asepsis, withdrawal and lack of contact : innocuous paper mediation in the resident toilet bowl according to the distant ideal of the blessèd and the saints whose residues, St. Bernard said, turn into a mild refined liquid, like balsam of frankincense and essence of myrrh : on the steep stairs that leads from stench to scent, from quadruped to angel via the act of excreting with neither fart nor fury : without dung, detritus or diarrhea : collective schizophrenia that today reaches its paroxysm in the orchestrated promotion of bleaches deodorants detergents destined to eliminate every guilty trace of the body's most obvious most crucial function : implacable merciless self-denial, the sickly stamp of which reveals the aggressive compensatory nature of omnivorous modern societies and their efficient repressive apparatus : coercion, rejection, veto, atrophy of the human organism brutally splitting it in two : upstairs : the visible, rational and tolerated : downstairs : the filthy, unspeakable and hidden : consequently, escape a similar fate, embark immediately and energetically on a salutary reconciliation with your body's hidden face and its private, most personal fruit : once and for all, put an end to the unhealthy intercession of toilet paper, reestablish manual contact : the age-old use of the water-can, the return to the humble yet dignified pleasures of evacuation in the public trench : the democratization you crave will thus be absolute, and, in case you are nostalgic for old-time unbridled consumerism, we've specially selected different models of portable washbasins, white or pastel shades, the ones we regularly advertise in the pages of *Elle* and *Le Jardin des Modes*

VI

seers
fortune-tellers
readers of entrails
soldiers in the ancient priestly caste

two opposing theories attempt to solve the problem : one subscribes to the well-rehearsed argument that the stage-sets and wardrobe are pure anachronism, cause for righteous indignation, a real school for scandal : that at the end of the day they're like everyone else and should dress similarly : the other assumes quite the contrary and reflects the views of the poets : on the contrary, emphasize difference and thus help the rabble to recognize them : cling to pomp and ceremony, gilded carriages and canopies, marble thrones and grandiose fans : insist on jesters' garb, force them to walk on stilts, increase the size of their headgear, lengthen their togas and extend their stovepipes : demand rituals and disguises from them and generally make them more vulnerable to finger-pointing and grins

VII

our inexorable enemy : the Little Couple curled up and glowing in their homey nest, happy and self-satisfied and, what's worse, keen to proliferate at a geometric rate and multiply over the face of the earth in step with the Creator's inept instructions : fount and origin of new hermetic cells in the beehive : of countless bland springy silk cocoons that symbolize their comfortable social status and voracious consumer appetites : lipstick, tissues, deodorants : Coca-Cola, ice-cold beer, scotch on the rocks : refrigerators, tape recorders, cars : holidays, psychiatrists, credit cards : gym, diets, anti-stress massages!
our cure? : very simple : an ars combinatoria of conflicting elements (individuals of every sex, race and age) in accord with the prin-

ciples governing artistic production (including imponderables like improvisation and games) : trios, quartets, quintets, septets, with light changing structures : avoiding the model of the self-absorbed little figures that illustrate bibliophile editions of the *Kama Sutra*, with their vertiginous rhythms worthy of the huge Taylorized factories in North America where copulation sadly apes production : embrace rather the elasticity of Calder's airy mobiles, their slender links obeying a secret many-sided current, forged from attractions and repulsions, centripetal and disintegrating forces : structures in fleeting precarious equilibrium, acrobatic, dancing, tightrope-walking, playful artisan virtuosity : magnetic field wherein continues the poet water-diviner's quest, with its subtle changes of rhythm and unusual associations : one style only banned : the logical-procreating kind : realm of semantic anomaly, of barren nonproductive bliss : pure pleasure, banned damned illicit venal

VIII

equally bitter enemy : offspring : ubiquitous all-devouring countless-headed hydra budding and surfacing unabashed in springtime after savage merciless pruning : repository of the vices and scourges of the old system, its contagious malevolent character transforming it into a virtually lethal adversary and demanding the harsh necessity of radical no-nonsense therapy : preventive slaughter of unholy innocents : methodically planned total elimination, no fucking qualms : buttando l'acqua sporca con il bambino and pulling the chain hard : measures sparing only bastard children of passion or ones who are the casual product of abominable forbidden love : thanks to Changó's rival's inspired decision, when he releases the beast shut up in the devil's amenable sibyl and lets it graze in a nearby shady spot authorized for visits by a Christian flock on festive days in order to ensure orderly propagation of the species : compelling it to go wild in that dingy spot and free its soul of sadness and sourness before returning to the hole open in the mother-of-pearl poetic cheeks of the body's hidden face : plebeian ancillary democratic : only these tangential marginal children, in whose hands we place the fate of our heroic invincible Revolution, deserve our support

IX

work-schedules? : none : means of subsistence? : those of the ritual potlatch economy : pillaging, theft, sacking of industrious neighboring towns, rollicking orgies lasting for months on end and, once the cycle's over and the prey consumed, off to war and back to the beginning

another caveat : the inclusion in our body of laws of a particularly forward-thinking clause aimed at protecting vagrants conceived by the unfairly sidelined son-in-law of that surly but altogether human prophet whose gloomy ominous predictions about Victorian capitalism would henceforth give sleepless nights to the drones who lived so agreeably on the product of their insect workers, forcing them to retrench into defensive, apparently generous and altruistic positions, subtly designed, in truth, as facts have since demonstrated, to disguise their rapacity and endlessly prolong their privileges : spawning on the rebound in vast but unfortunately autocratic and backward countries those egalitarian societies that, taking inspiration from his vague model, and thanks to the phenomenal organizational skills of this efficient, modern-day Saul, put an end to the old form of exploitation, but not to work itself : communities forced to produce and create wealth to resist the economic siege mounted by their adversaries and, as a result of the deep-rooted natural tendency to make a virtue out of necessity and lurch from putting their best foot forward to an almost Job-like acceptance of evil as a kind of cheery slap on the back from fate, compelled to embrace as exemplary and paradigmatic the behavior of the submissive castrated scab who proudly stacks up unpaid overtime : alienated brain, perfect hymenoptera, nonetheless dubbed a new hero by the grim mustachioed patriarch who ceremoniously plastered him in medals on the podium of the blossoming supreme leadership : an instructive episode we always bring to mind when the budgerigars and parrots of our two-headed productive society lambaste our playful tendencies and vibrant praise of vagabondage : we have banished once and for all the process of accumulation and have not yielded to the sophistry of those perpetuating it on behalf of a remote paradise : we act in the present moment, which is our only concern : reclaiming the leisure that Santiago's Moor (Pauline in name alone) urged : fomenting gambling, recreation, and dissipation : and condemning work, you bet, and without appeal

X

it's vital to decide, stats in hand, who silently and cynically makes off with the ant's humble surplus value : is it the hidebound cicada

130

absorbed in her random repetitive resonant chores? : or the venal individualistic grasshopper who tirelessly hoards for the pure
pleasure of hoarding? : most accuse the bumblebee of playing the
middleman, the would-be protector of a remote nebulous queen :
the cricket's role is also up for debate, and some speak of conclusive
evidence : resolutions and papers demand the dragonfly implement
a clear precise program of action : fondness for the flowery arouses
suspicion, and isn't flashy dressing an anachronism in these hard
times of struggle and sacrifice? : the glowworm has its detractors
: its elite, nighttime conspiratorial activities apparently lose it a lot
of sympathizers : finally, some accuse the ants themselves and their
love of work : if they folded their arms and did fuck all, so they say,
nobody could live on their surplus value

XI

repression? : none whatsoever : we believe the community is di-
rectly responsible for an individual's delinquent acts and, rather
than sanctioning the latter as in the old scheme of things, we believe it to be more logical to amend society itself : how? : by hit-
ting it where it hurts most, to force it to adopt corrective measures
and avoid in the future the injustices that usually foment criminal
activity : by destroying, say, its most famous monuments or the
symbols of a glorious past : devastating the cathedrals of Cologne
or Canterbury, Notre-Dame de Paris or the Duomo in Milan : rip-
ping up the most renowned canvasses in the British Museum or
the Louvre, the Prado or Galleria Borghese : blowing up the Pietà
or Dama de Elche, the Arc de Triomphe or the Statue of Liberty :

not forgetting to exhume the remains of some literary or scientific genius, illustrious peer or father of the nation in a carefully staged ceremony : summon the entire populace opposite the Pantheon and while a drum rolls remove the urn containing the sacrosanct ashes, process silently with it to the nearest river, stop by the Bridge of Sighs, allow a minute for tears and sobs, and throw the ashes majestically into the flow as one does the bodies of sailors deceased on the high seas : last year we thus rid ourselves of the bones of Manzoni, Kipling and Victor Hugo (to mention but a few) : this year, deeply saddened, we watched those of George Washington, Garibaldi, and Bismarck disappear : and who knows whether destiny might hold even more grievous losses in store! : Napoleon, Metternich, Catherine of Russia? : Pasteur, Edison, Ramón y Cajal? : even so, a meager if sincere consolation reconciles us with all this sadness : crime doesn't increase, as in the two-sided productive society and, according to the calculations by the Institute for Statistics, after decreasing year after year in a geometrical regression, crime itself will become extinct in the following decade

XII

other goals anticipated by the aforementioned body : spectacular increase (both in quantitative and qualitative terms) of sinister sterile copulations (at the expense of the productive love of former class-based societies) : right to leisure extended to the entire citizenry : free exhibition (through open flaps in the backs of skirts or seats of pants) of those wonderful convexities whose unique ineffable eyes magnify and enhance the shy nether face : a few warts as well

: alarming reduction in the number of livestock, regrettable neglect of traditional pastures : but violent appropriation of the surplus value of our neighbors (that is, of the fruits of their unrelenting toil) more than compensating for their shortfalls and restoring the balance in our favor : on the other hand (and we should make this quite clear), we will not defend any elitist criteria as regards flora and fauna : we equally support all animal and vegetable species, even those that men, throughout history, in their hateful egocentrism, have decreed harmful and useless : now bedbugs, fleas and other parasites live peacefully on us in the same way we live on edible goods from the soil : following the venerable Ibn Turmeda's guidelines, we have democratized the hierarchy of animals and no longer consider ourselves the lords and masters of anyone, as we used to : species formerly seen as vile and loathsome now flourish untrammeled in our society and, with fraternal attentions, we encourage the reproduction of all manner of reptiles and especially the hatedfeared snakes : their numbers are expanding and, according to the most reliable predictions, huge voracious specimens will gradually infiltrate the biped family hearth and stealthily slither into the matrimonial bed, no less

XIII

Michelet tells it straight in his renowned History
    c'est sous cette bannière de modération et de justice in-
    dulgente que s'inaugura le lendemain la nouvelle religion :
    Gossec avait fait les chants, Chénier les paroles : on avait,
    tant bien que mal, en deux jours, bâti dans le choeur, fort

étroit, de Notre-Dame, un temple à la Philosophie,
qu'ornaient les effigies des sages, des pères de la Révolu-
tion : une montagne portait le temple : sur un rocher
brûlait le flambeau de la Vérité : les magistrats siégeaient
sous les colonnes : point d'armes, point de soldats : deux
rangs de jeunes filles encore enfants faisaient tout
l'ornement de la fête : elles étaient en robes blanches, cou-
ronnées de chêne, et non, comme on l'a dit, de roses
la Raison, vêtue de blanc avec un manteau d'azur, sort
du temple de la Philosophie, vient d'asseoir sur un siège de
simple verdure : les jeunes filles lui chantent son hymne :
elle traverse au pied de la montagne en jetant sur
l'assistance un doux regard, un doux sourire : elle rentre,
et l'on chante encore : on attendait : mais c'était tout
chaste cérémonie, triste, sèche, ennuyeuse!
we won't be guilty of such a crass error : on the ruins of churches and
ideologies, we will surrender to the rapturous pleasures of the clandestine nocturnal worship of the dangerous gorilla from the movies
and his explicitly paradigmatic categorically imperious COB

VI

in the deep silence of the study-kitchen the moth flutters around
the lamp : gyrates, glides, obsessively describes circles, flies off
when you frighten it only to return immediately, again and again
and again, to the glow that fascinates and attracts, absorbed by its
lunatic endeavors, scornful of your swipes : likewise, from the moment you come back from the bathroom, the reiterated phantom
idea surges and attacks, fades when you rebuff it, insistent stubborn and mute, confident of eventual victory, knowing you will
tire straightaway: so you resign yourself and welcome it : solitude
favors its flight and the parallel is quite clearly posited : why would
you still resist tracing it?

tantalized, beginning your own personal examination of the canon
of the novel and x-raying its smug exponents : while you grope for
the secret will o' the wisp equation that surreptitiously combines
sexuality and writing : your fondness for grasping your pen and
letting its liquid thread run, indefinitely prolonging orgasm

*

you will glide airily over wondrous tropical isles, haven and shelter to
your painful childhood : yours? : no, the other's : the prissy (later executed) infant driven by ecumenical desires to proselytize, by frantic
longings to regenerate : dressed in snow-white like the Petits Frères
of the similarly martyred Révérend Père de Foucauld : in (white) sou-

tane and with colonial (also white) pith helmet harmoniously contrasting with the dark complexion and muddy bodies of the hapless indigenous peoples deprived by heavenly decree of the grandiose benefits of Redemption : offering blessings, advice, alms, soothing smiles, sweet words of consolation : helping widows, giving succor to orphans, freeing slaves : surrounded by a bevy of African children, tout noirs, oui, mais doux et intelligents : the shoulders of fleet-of-foot coolies support the light palankeen, with its immaculate canopy, in which he travels and a slender catechumen fans him gracefully flourishing a pay-pay : in one of the countries of the apostolate minutely described in magazines the pious holy family subscribed to : as soon as he (the other) is resting behind the innocent veil of his mosquito net his lady-in-waiting and maids think he's asleep and scrutinize his toy priest's kit muttering approvingly and fawningly to one another

the little angel's just celebrated mass

yesterday he said he wanted to be a missionary

and he's always looking at the map of Africa!

just look, a little saint

shush, don't wake him up!

yes, he has the calling

(he) savoring within (himself) the delights of victory : conferring divine grace on myriad children otherwise condemned to miserable monotonous limbo or awful eternal punishments : always wearing a mobile weightless halo like those in your books of pious prints as he explores savannahs, jungles and steppes, greeted by the applause of the cheering natives who kneel down and kiss his redeeming priestly ring

*

the magnificats and antiphons of the faithful round off the gradual
transformation of the area, and the smell of incense from his childhood (the other's, the dead one's) will swirl insidiously around the
queue of penitents almost a quarter of a century ago
anything else, kid?
well, you say, I also didn't keep the sixth
the sixth? he exclaims
right, the sixth!
once or repeatedly?
endlessly!
in deed or in thought?
in deed and in thought!
alone or accompanied?
alone and accompanied!
with men or with women?
with men and with women!
with children? he mutters
with little boys! and little girls! with old ladies! and old men!
that's impossible, he groans
oh no, it's not, you shout : with anything that moves!
oh my God!
with dogs! with goats! with swans! with dromedaries!
cunnilingus?
cunnilingus!
immissio in anum?
immissio in anum!
coitus inter femora?

coitus inter femora!

fellatio?

fellatio!

ejaculatio praematura?

ejaculatio praemutura!

receptaculum seminis?

receptaculum seminis!

the wretched priest will cross himself repeatedly : the terrible visions in your tale seem to have disturbed his mind and, struggling hard to assert violent self-control, he will address the Mistress of the Sugar-Mill in the Sky in halting tones, interrupted by sudden convulsions : but on this occasion, Little Fermina doesn't take a flask of smelling salts from her corsage or cover her ears in horror : her smiling eyes, delicately drawn by the artificer, wince, visibly nauseated, and pointing the thumb of her right hand at the ground, like emperors at a Roman circus, she will very clearly indicate that in her opinion he's an incurable case, and that for everybody's good, particularly for that of the apoplectic half-choking Father, it's best to stop being namby-pamby and sentimental and get rid of the guilty party as soon as possible

stripped of Changó's resplendent majesty, you will offer up to the unpolluted Common Mother the first fruits of your poetic offering

labyrinth of errors

ora pro nobis!

fearful desert

ora pro nobis!

abode of savage beasts

ora pro nobis!

lake full of slime
ora pro nobis!
stony ground
ora pro nobis!
meadow full of serpents
ora pro nobis
flowering garden without fruit
ora pro nobis!
fount of sorrows
ora pro nobis!
river of tears
ora pro nobis!
sea of woe
ora pro nobis!
toil without profit
ora pro nobis!
sweet poison
ora pro nobis!
vain hope
ora pro nobis!
false happiness
ora pro nobis!
a real Queen Kong

                          *

if you were condemned to stay shut inside a dark room, completely sealed off, unable to see the smallest ray of light, with nowhere you could ever hope to rest

if the floor were littered with broken glass, brambles bristling with thorns, where snakes slithered and constantly bit you and flames licked all around, and not for a day or a week, but your whole lifetime, wouldn't you find the very thought horrific? right then, Hell is much more terrible and lasts the whole of eternity

*

to the park, in a hurry, running to the park, holding the hand of a wet-nurse or deceased lady-in-waiting, down remote paths covered in a very fine gravel, snaking between flowerbeds and clipped hedges, passing by little rustic bridges, arbors, bandstands, ponds, statues, on to the meeting point where the other children shout, fight, jump, make sand castles, swing, go down slides and meet up with the nuns who titter furiously, whirl around in their starched wimples, organize games of hide and seek leapfrog hopscotch dancing competitions, and circle round him like butterflies from some giant extinct species and der Mutter invites him to join the cheerful group who are singing, a littel anngree vith yar frendz, no?, in her unmistakable Teutonic accent, no vehrry fond of dar platime gamess, trying to puncture his conceit and self-absorption, ahh pliz repeat afder me, villy, villy, ach so pretty, vither do yar vander, vatch out for der vitch vanting to rob yar, bending over him to get him to sing the chorus, villy villy, and pinching his arm hard, ach, dass yar veel it, I bet yar dass now and t'en? yar like play mumz and dadz az vell? visper in my ear, t'ese t'ingz verri nasti, if the porr Viggin seez ya ach she vill cut off yar villy

✳

solitary pleasure of writing!

gently flourishing the pen, stroking it like a sweaty adolescent
in that drowsiness that encourages manual playfulness, letting
the liquid thread leak onto the blank page, attaining a soloist's
delicate perfection, your subtle artifice prolonging the stiffness
of your menhir, indefinitely deferring orgasm, consuming your
own energy, unbridled, banishing the stubborn miserliness of
propriety : surrendering to the aleatory inspiration guiding your
footsteps on your Sunday and holiday strolls : when like a falcon circling over its prey, you walk in the labyrinths of the urban
jungle like a swift sharp-eyed peregrine : reacting to the magnetic
pull of the body that irresistibly attracts yours and couples with
you, strong and compact like words joined by the poet in versatile
fleeting combinations : transforming semantic deviations into a
voltaic spark, spurning logic's cheap disdain : until the moment
when parallel quests converge, the word becomes flesh, and loving copulation dazzles like a resplendent metaphor : scorning the
ominously close-at-hand religious social-realist or psychological
critic who, poised over the trench of scholarly learning, waves an
accusing finger at the little shrine and bellows that he has witnessed a mutually consenting act devoted to Onan : the abominable act of flourishing the pen without profit to the general public
and its multiple urgent needs : a chorus goes up from virtuously
indignant righteous folk who are peering out of their windows
and watching this spectacle of human scum in action, bawling
and shouting, terrified yet fascinated
oh, comme c'est dégoûtant!

141

take a look

it turns my stomach

disgraziato!

monsieur, vous n'avez pas honte?

execute them, execute them, sí señor!

quick, snap it!

please don't move

regarde, il jouit!

tío guarro!

un momentino, per carità

look at this

andiamo, è troppo orrido!

when the babelian crowd scatters, the Faithful Disciple will gaze up at the Mistress of the Sugar-Mill in the Sky and Little Fermina will furrow her brow and once more point the thumb of her right hand at the ground like Caesar after gladiatorial combat indicating very clearly that in her opinion the case is incurable and for the general good and particularly for the health of the novel, its ideologues and stipendiary sentinels, it is best to stop being namby-pamby and sentimental and put an end to you right now, you recalcitrant obscene sinner

*

as the weasel voice turns hysterical and grates disagreeably in your ears, you'll rehearse the same spare gesture of the Mistress of the Sugar-Mill in the Sky and point the thumb of your right hand at the ground, like emperors at a Roman circus : at once its tone rises and reaches the pitch of screams that cattle let rip when taken to the slaughterhouse : but luckily it will soon stop and when you put your pen down and get up to take a pee, this time it will be Our Lady in Heaven, alias Little Fermina, who, without sorrow or glory, will have definitively gone to the wall

VII

Now I am fearless, a man with nothing
to lose, a man who finds your company
irksome, like a poor wayfarer who walks
and sings at the top of his voice, unafraid of
cruel brigands.

Fernando de Rojas, *Celestina*

eliminate the last traces of theatricality from the corpus of the novel
: transform it into an uneventful discourse : dynamite the worn-out
notion of the flesh-and-blood character : replacing the dramatic
progression of the story with clusters of text driven by a single centripetal force : organizing kernel of the writing itself, pen fountain-
ing the textual process : improvising the architecture of the literary
object not as a tissue of relationships ordered by time and logic
but as an ars combinatoria of elements (oppositions, alternatives,
symmetrical play) on the rectangle of the blank page : emulating
painting and poetry at a purely spatial level : indifferent to the vo-
ciferous or tacit threats of the commissar-sergeant-customs-officer
disguised as a critic : deaf to the siren songs of self-interested func-
tional-content based and petty utilitarian criteria

*

Good Friday : or Man Friday? : on the blank endlessly virginal
rectangle, the pen dizzily faces a double incitement (error, trick?)

: arbitrariness of the story always disguised under false pretenses : sitting on (under?) your picnic table, frozen by the opaque ray of sunlight crossing the massive wall : sign evoking (valid assumption) the rainy day that scorches, the fertile Antarctic landscape, thirsty as a steppe : heavily planted streets and avenues, stone sycamores, gardens watered by taxis and trams : pen in mouth, bullets (words) winging multiple possible perspectives : restrictive cause and effect, mean-spirited determinism of a sad bird in the hand preferred to the inebriation of hundreds airborne : logical actions, coherent syntax, exhausted bloodless inventions of a worn-out Old Testament Jehovah! : dreaming of the boundless pleasure of the capricious and unlikely : infinite universe of the improbable where unreason blossoms and enthralling chaos smears the whiteness of the page with an enigmatic and liberating proliferation of signs

*

autonomy of the literary object : verbal structure with its own inner connections, language perceived in itself and not as a transparent mediator of an alien external world : via the act of releasing words from their subjugation to a pragmatic order that transforms them into mere vehicles of almighty reason : of logical thought that uses them contemptuously without considering their specific weight and worth : fulfilling the functions of representation, expression and address inherent in oral communication whose elements (transmitter, receiver, context, contact) also operate (though diversely) at the moment of reading in a fourth (erogenous?) function that will exclusively center attention on the linguistic sign : thanks to that, stripping language of its ancillary miserly purpose : transmuting semantic anomaly into a kernel for generating poetry and at a stroke, combining, in polysemic harmony, sexuality and writing : general contempt for the useful procreating serial mode that changes abominable barren pleasure into a figure of speech, the crimine pessimo into existential metaphor : at last resolving, at the end of such a long a detour, the secret equation of your double deviation : nonproductive (onanistic) manipulation of the written word, self-sufficient (poetic) exercise in illicit pleasuring

*

you will reproduce once again, in your neat hand, the slave's letter, a reading of which clarifies and gives meaning to a life (yours?) organized (as a result of the letter) in an uninterrupted process of rupture, of casting away, knowing that you possess the key to interpreting his journey (the other's) retrospectively, conscious you have reached the end of a cycle and that, from now on, skin changed and debts paid, you can live in peace

     my master

     your 'onor left me in the 'ouse of your children little Fermina and little Jorgito and I did every t'ing possible to keep my promise to your 'onor but when little Telesfora came to little Ferminita's 'ouse they chucked me out so I'm out on the street like that waitin' always for your 'onor

     I can also tell your 'onor that little Telesfora did sell Julián to Tomabella and Tomabella did sell him to Montalvo and since the summer your son Jorgito won't give him even 'alf a cent

     please your 'onor do somet'ing 'cos this poor t'ing's nuttin' to eat I 'ope your 'onor 'elp me

best wishes to Petra María little Flora little Ángeles little
Josefita and to my mistress
and your 'onor bid your slave who begs 'is blessing
Casilda Mendiola
cry of pain
secret source of the liberating process of your pen
hidden reason for your ethical artistic social religious and sexual
deviation

*

ten years back, in the space of your own writing
the Great Souk opened before you, vast multicolored polychrome,
with its dark awnings, stalls, bazaars, attacked by a blistering sun
and from the incomprehensible chatter of unlettered traders and
tinny tinkling of water-sellers' little bells, you picked out the voice
of that woman, or rather her accent, distilled product, you might
say, of sluggish centuries of stable order, hierarchical sense of duty,
well-honed awareness of control, blind faith in smoothly-function-
ing laws wisely governing the destinies of the world
get out the way, Paco, he'll touch you!
you turned round to see who'd spoken that way, the sickening Sansueña good-looker, dressed up, spruced up, dyed, embellished by
cloths, perfumes, eyeliner, lacquers naturally purchased in high-
class boutiques on the Faubourg Saint-Honoré by a husband sporting a lantern jaw, Bourbon nose, perfectly horizontal little mus-
tache shaped like the tilde atop the ñ, eyes veiled by sunglasses with
thick tortoiseshell frames that cover the sides like the blinkers of a
horse

fucking assholes, you opined

(in front of them, and of you, too, an Arab beggar, age indefinite, body apparently host to all the blights and defects of the human species

filthy

dirt-poor

suppurating

sores)

if only, you told yourself, I could inspire similar loathing, gather to myself the same abjection, vileness, hideous sores able to spark the righteous contempt of this fetid pair

and like the bare twisted almond tree suddenly and miraculously blossoming in the icy depths of January, the beggar was transformed for you into a lovely symbol of desire, his previous ugliness transmuted by an alchemist's mold into the apex and acme of astonishing beauty

you knew from then on that no ethics, no philosophy, no aesthetic would be valid for the flock tamed by five centuries of conformity if it didn't dare risk provoking the couple's same shrieks of disgust at the sight of the scabby scrounger beggar

deliberately laughable

willfully shocking

fleeing the snares and ploys of a sick-making respectability

independent furrow, life on the margin

sooner or later, you thought

(and still think)

some people would, perhaps, understand

*

monotone or accidental? compared by some to a scratched record, the history of your one-time fatherland also evokes Ravel's interminable bolero

in the drawing-rooms of the prefecture in Bayonne, the old département of the Basses Pyrénées, the immortal pretenders to the throne display their coats-of-arms and titles to conceited hoodlum holding letters of marque : their family pedigree is excellent and apparently flatters the snobbery of the ambitious maître de maison : the Cid figures here, naturally, and the grumpy hillsman Don Pelayo : one man invokes his consanguinity with Túbal : another declares Wamba was his uncle and Sancho the Wild was his cousin, remember? : bright red tinges the peacocks' victory, chatterbox Sansueña mouths commonplaces while the Bourbon goes native in a kilt century after century the chroniclers debate these heraldic games and spread confusion and doubt in the logical Cartesian mind of your old concierge on the Rue Poissonnière

monsieur, par charité, où va l'Espagne?

à sa perte, j'espère

*

your body won't fertilize the soil of that land : unless, aided by a powerful noxious substance, it can spread its parasitic undermining action to the whole expanse of the Peninsula, gradually polluting the national tree of literature, till it withers like that ill-fated contorted fig tree the Bible castigates so roundly : but if reality doesn't bow to your oneiric assault you'll have to decide right now what fate to hold in reserve : the latest graduate from la Puebla, your name will never honor inaugurations of schools statues squares avenues boulevards : birds won't settle on your laurels, dogs won't sully your plinth, cheerful childish voices won't voice your syllables

149

: evicted, beyond the pale, no one but no one will reclaim your remains : sparing an obscene symbiosis with that abominable land, you will let them repose in the calm of a Muslim makbara : among the crowd of stones eroded by insatiable gusts of wind : prudent geometry of curves and rough edges, snaking dunes that caress and stifle in voracious serpentine sifting embrace : completely melt into the barren sand : finally integrated into a sterile landscape : unless, like the needy on your native plot in the years following the grim catastrophe, you sell the thing to a cadaver wholesaler or clinical hospital for future medics to test and practice on, men able in their time to successfully diagnose the reasons for centuries-long collective constipation

*

completed now the cycle of biological evolution changing the larva into a seemingly lovely shiny insect, aloof, back turned on its hazy origins
like a batrachian whose spectacular series of transmutations are neither accompanied nor followed by any moral apothegms
like Proteus, Fregoli or a transvestite performing to an audience, simultaneously mocking and mocked
you have transformed yourself and transformed the instrument you use to express yourself, offloading on each sheet of white paper the shreds and tatters of your former personality until you reached the present state when only a nominal flimsy façade identifies you like that tetchy alienated evasive old woman who pulled the shutters down on her previous life and ceased to recognize her own family and now only retains a veneer of politeness that allows im-

personal exchanges and conversations with her fretful grandson as
if he were a stranger in a doctor's waiting room
that's you now, after a taxing sequence of changes and metamor-
phoses, at the inevitable autumnal moment to make your melancholy farewells
apostasies, transgressions, exile have distanced you forever from
the native fauna and the urbane formulae you occasionally swap
with them are as mechanical and vapid as grandmother's washed-
out smile on the memorable day when she didn't recognize him
no, not you
that other whose changes of skin signal warily, tom-thumbishly,
along the way, the gains and risks of his proud and solitary betrayal

*

if you write in future, it will be in another language : not the one
you've rejected and that today you say goodbye to after turning
it upside down, undercutting and stunning it : an inner seditious
endeavor rewarded by the gift you offer very much in spite of
yourself : adding your artifact to its monument, but at the same
time distilling the (caustic corrosive mordant) agent that corrupts
and wears it down : captious gift (yours) like a scorpion's tail : (its)
tricky offering with in cauda venenum : ambiguous relationship
that kept you from sleeping until its abrupt deviation reached a
logical conclusion : the release of the instrument and vehicle of
your (its) own rupture : knowing that from that moment you (it)
can sleep peacefully : with a clear conscience, the evil deed is done
: vile progeny, (your) (ideological narrative semantic) subversion
will independently pursue its underhand labors : for ever and ever

*

get unfamiliar with your language this very minute, start writing it according to mere phonetic intuition without the go a hed of Dayme Akademee onlee to continyu with t' rite lingo of milliuns of men and wimmin who natter in it everyday not never thinkin' about the peenal grammer imposed by ther manderin', forgittin' bit by bit all they learnt yer in a cleresited go at iliteracee wot'll tek yer ter pun'o' rejectin'won ater anuther t' wird' o' yer lingo an' replacin' t'em wid turms ledin' yer to ayrab eli tebdá tadrus chuya-b-chuya, lugha uára bissaf ualakini eli thabb bissaf, knowin' thart fr'm naron lassmék t-takalem mesyan ila tebghi tsáfar men al bildan mesel-mas ua tebghi taáref ahsán er-rájal wot inspired yer buke but'll not never rede it, ráxel min Uxda Tenira Uahran Ghasauet El-Asnam Tanxa Dar-Lyfe hooz cumpanee giv' yer gud nolige o' yessen' an' t' chanse ter ken it freein' yer fr'm yer preevius posin' an', t'anks t'er practisin' a bodilingo o' t'wird woz trulee med flesh, o' tebdá kif uáhed láarbi al idu sghera ua min baád al idu Kbira temxi l-xaama u etkará al surat li thhab

الناس لي ماينصموش مايبقاوش يتبعوني

علاقتنا انتهت

أنا بدون شك في الجهة الأخرى

مع المساكين لي دائما

يوجدوا السكين

Afterword to the New Edition of *Juan the Landless*

Juan Goytisolo

I have always rejected the term "experimental" in relation to my novels following *Marks of Identity*. Every work that aspires to be innovative does just that, experiment, but its contribution to the tree of literature can't be reduced to a simple laboratory test: form and material should be a tight fit, and their ideal symbiosis go unnoticed to whoever accepts the challenge and adventure of a reading. That is the case with *Count Julian* as well as the novels written from *Makbara* onward. But in the case of *Juan the Landless*, my wish to break with artistic, social, intellectual, and moral conformism doesn't entirely succeed in fusing betrayal as theme and betrayal as language; the latter is too visible, and undermines the desirable unity of the book.

My rereading of the novel opened my eyes to a theoretical overload, particularly in the third and sixth chapters of the first edition, and I have now removed a good number of pages. I think this pruning or slimming-cure lightens the text and brings a greater unity of composition. The doctrinal pressure exerted by some of the mandarins of the Left Bank, which Severo Sarduy experienced and resisted as best he could, had a passing influence on me in the years 1965–1975, when I was reading widely in the Russian Formalists, the Prague Circle, Benveniste, Bakhtin, the Tartu School, and Noam Chomsky. The third chapter of *Juan the Landless* suffers from sequences or sub-chapters that are entirely or partly unnecessary ("hairottomaniacs," "the eighth pillar of wisdom," "incursions into

Nubian territory," "variations on a Fez theme," "in the footsteps of Father Foucauld"), in which the *you* of the narrator identifies with individuals like Lawrence of Arabia, the sanctimonious founder of the White Fathers, or Anselm Turmeda, whose single common denominator was a fascination with Islam. Digressions—the preferred method of going round the houses—may amuse and stimulate if handled with artistic ingenuity—*Tristram Shandy* is a magnificent example of precisely that—providing the novelist turns these into the backbone that structures the entire narrative where they are embedded. But not everyone can be a Sterne and leaps across the jungle like by a Tarzan clinging to a liana can end in crash-landings, and their gratuitousness or pedantry will only annoy the reader.

I like the sequences I've eliminated, with the sole exception of "hairottomaniacs." However, I prefer them to be read as independent pieces. Their idiosyncratic and anachronistic meandering, behind changing masks, through the Sahara, North Africa, Nubia, or Jordan, excised from the present and definitive version of *Juan the Landless*, are printed at the end of the third volume of my *(In) Complete Works*, in a narrative miscellany of unconnected texts. As for chapter six of the first edition, which contains the most theorizing in the novel—the parodies of Professor Vosk, whom only my former students at New York University could identify—constitute heavy stodge the reader can well do without. The good Professor, and others of his species, have well earned their relegation to oblivion.

Stripped now of its excesses, the violence of *Juan the Landless* is starker, and this heightened tension imbues the whole of the writing. Its uniqueness provokes a feeling of strangeness in the general reader: I know of no other book in Spanish literature that has these features. If I must seek a precedent—another jubilant hymn to Evil—I find it in the same pages where the destructive poetic rage of some of the surrealists found inspiration. Obviously, I'm thinking of *Les Chants de Maldoror* by Isidore Ducasse, the Count of Lautré-amont, and a neighbor of mine in my *arrondissement* in Paris. The first chapter in the novel serves as the thread binding the others, and is the one I like most. The return to the scenario of the sugar-mills and plantations that belonged to my Cuban forebears, prompted by the LP cover of a 33 RPM record by the "raunchy fat lady"—my much-lamented Celia Cruz—and the pages of the masterpiece by the historian Moreno Fraginals on the island's sugarocracy and the system of slavery on which it was based, begins with the burlesque scene with great-grandfather-God and Little Fermina-the-Virgin-Mary, and her dialogue with the priest on the subject of their slave-holdings.

When I was writing the book my only aids were the letters from slaves and the faded yellowing photos of great-grandfather's sugarmills, the Goytisolo and Montalvo sugarcane train and the corvette *Flora*, which were preserved until 1985 in the old family property in Torrentbó and had already been mentioned or reproduced in the first chapter of *Marks of Identity*. The essay recently published by the researcher Martín Rodrigo y Alharilla, of the Pompeu Fabra University in Barcelona, on the sugar plantations built and run by my ancestors, includes valuable information on how these worked and made their profits. The purchase of African slaves and Chinese coolies, the acquisition of new land and the way the wealth accumulated was channeled to Barcelona—at the time, the engine of Spain's incipient industrialization—are described by the protagonists themselves, who were extremely worried by the rebellion of the *mambises* and black runaway slaves, and thus decided to invest their fortune in the capital of Catalonia. The correspondence between my great-uncle Agustín Fabián and my grandfather Antonio are not to be missed, especially when read in tandem with the really shocking letters from the slaves.

One of their exchanges inspired some thoughts I published in *Babelia* on September 11, 2004, under the title "The Conspiracy of Chance":

> Reason wrestles with determinism and chance. Our existence shifts between the two poles, never choosing either. In modern times, philosophers, from Pascal to Kierkegaard, have confronted the dilemma without resolving it. In two stories in *The Aleph*, Borges describes the extent of the problem better than anyone: "There is no fact, however humble it may be, that is not implicated in universal history and its infinite concatenation of causes and effects [...], that is so vast and so intimate that perhaps not a single fact, however insignificant, could be erased, without invalidating the present. To modify the past is not to modify a single fact: it is to erase its consequences, and they tend to be infinite."

Recently, when I was reading the essay by Professor Martín Rodrigo y Alharilla on the financial vicissitudes of my Basque-Cuban ancestors ("From Landowners in Cienfuegos to Investors in Barcelona," *Revista de Historia Industrial*, 23), I found irrefutable proof of the correctness of the above observation by Borges. The author reprints some letters my paternal great-uncle Agustín Fabián sent to my grandfather Antonio, where he advises him to marry the woman who would then become my grandmother, Catalina Taltavull: "You look after yourself, marry a well-off girl, and don't try to make money on the Stock Exchange, because you'll only get a battering you never bargained for"; and in a later letter, "If you're thinking of getting married, make sure lots of cash is involved, because that's what you need in life. So go for it. And what about this Taltavull girl?"

From the moment I began to reason and ask questions about the world and my appearance in it, I'd never seen the concatenation of chances behind my own existence so clearly: I was born, have lived, and am who I am because of those letters from November 1881! Thanks to them, my grandfather Antonio married that sweet, bright, and distant Catalina Taltavull, whose beautiful portrait as a melancholic adolescent I often contemplate, and who was impregnated a dozen times—ten boys and girls survived—by her very disinterested husband, and died in childbirth before reaching the age of forty. The erasure of this distant, apparently nondescript fact would invalidate the existence of several generations of my family, a product of that "conspiracy of chance" that Scheherazade mentions.

I immediately thought: what would have happened if these letters had never reached their destination? If the boat carrying them had sunk? If an unscrupulous postman had stolen them? Ladies and gentlemen, I would not exist and, consequently, neither would you, at least as readers of the lines you're now perusing. Without the judicious advice from my great-uncle, his letters, their transportation by sea to Barcelona, and arrival in the hands of the recipient, none of all the good or bad I have done would ever have happened.

The Bakhtinian scene when the English engineers are installing the WC or clean aseptic toilet, where the owners of the sugar-mill sublimate their feces in front of "the niggers," goes back to my readings of Norman Brown and Octavio Paz, a sentence by whom—"the face distanced itself from the ass," taken from *Conjunctions and Disjunctions*—figures as a quotation at the beginning of *Juan the Landless*. This technological gadget to conceal our animal nature would thus allow

> the non-material invisible odorless perfect emission which, thanks to rear flaps, plummets down the double cavity to the central cistern, that vault of riches, immaculate and aseptic as a bank's

A thousand leagues from those

> de-surplus-valued blacks of the common trench, in direct contact with coarse matter, vile excretions, viscerally plebian emanations

The implicit parallel between defecation and the sexual act, whether solitary or not, and the heroic efforts by the boy Alvarito, encouraged by the Master of the Sugar-Mill in the Sky and the White Virgin, expended on not defecating in his china chamber pot, provide the thread underpinning the remaining chapters of the book. The concealing of the act of excretion and the chastity imposed or regulated by the Church are two faces of the same coin: the futile aspiration towards the angelic that sours the lives of Catholic believers and drags them into a repeated cycle of sin-confession-sin by a Rome which thus asserts its domination. Adolescent sexuality is as natural and irrepressible as the act of defecating, and Alvarito will never be a saint, a halo in motion, as The Master Up Above and the White Virgin want. The public trench of the Arabs and blacks irresistibly attracts the *you* of the narrator and narrative and leads him through the various episodes in the book, from King Kong's New York to the African desert, from great-grandfather's slaves to the Nubians, from the fallacious casuistry of the "biped species" to the adoration of the slinking slithering snake. His surrender to the pariahs and the abominable pleasure they bring won't transmute him into a blessèd being or new man but into a member of the horde taking its revenge on the hypocrisy of the world. His voice will thus be the voice of the body, of verbal imagination and mortal and artistic transgression:

> listen carefully to what we say
> the traps set by your logic won't catch us
> morality
> religion
> society
> patriotism
> family
> are threatening noises and their sonorous clatter leave us
>   indifferent
> don't count on us
> we believe in a world without frontiers
> wandering Jews

heirs to John Lackland
we'll set up camp where our instinct leads us
the Agarene community attracts us and we'll take refuge
   there
forget that same old story
the hackneyed threat of shameful ruins and catastrophes
après nous le déluge?
WE SHALL SOW TEMPESTS!

After the supplications to the African gods of the Abakua and the Lucumis in Cuba and the reciting of the *ora pro nobis* of devotion to Mary intercalated in Pleberio's soliloquy in *Celestina*, the recrimination against the World by its author Fernando de Rojas with which I begin my public readings of the dialogue with the demiurge from *The Blind Rider*, will cast its lucid shadow over the final chapter:

> *Now I am fearless, a man with nothing to lose, a man who finds your company irksome, like a poor wayfarer who walks and sings at the top of his voice, unafraid of cruel brigands.*

The destructive endeavors of *Count Julian* and *Juan the Landless* end here and, from now on, Spain—a "stain on the map"—will disappear from the horizon in the majority of my novels and become, conversely, the undoubted protagonist in my books of essays. The peremptory declaration made by the *you* invoked in *Juan the Landless* "if you write in the future, it will be in another language: not the one you have rejected and that today you bid farewell to after turning it upside down, undercutting and stunning it," and the dissolving of the latter, first into phonetic colloquial Cuban and then the North African dialect of Arabic, were interpreted by some as my farewell to Spanish and my death as a Spanish writer. More modestly, I was referring to the dispossession or uprooting necessary in order to start from scratch and be reborn without the restrictions imposed by the social, moral, and aesthetic order that was the product of oppressive indoctrination in my youth: to move on to a counter-education and self-taught cycle of learning that has yet to end. Life and literature are different realities: flesh doesn't resuscitate. The only genuine death/resurrection exists in the ambit of literature and nowhere else.

The last page in Arabic characters brings the general reader up against a dead end. It's an abrupt way of saying goodbye and shutting the book on him. The short text I composed in *Darisha* was transcribed in a better hand than mine by a New York Arabist, and means the following:

> If you don't understand,
> stop following me.
> Communication between us is ended.
> I've gone definitively over to the other side,
> with the eternal pariahs,
> sharpening my knife.

Juan the Landless stopped there and I continued on my way.

From Obras Completas III: Juan Goytisolo Novelas (1966–1982). *Barcelona: Galaxia Gutenberg, 2006.*

Translated by Peter Bush

Born in 1931, JUAN GOYTISOLO went into voluntary exile in 1956 and has never returned to live in Spain. A bitter opponent of the Franco regime, his early novels, including *Marks of Identity*, were banned in Spain. He divided his time between Paris and Marrakesh until the death of his wife, Monique Lange, at which time he moved permanently to Marrakesh. He is the author of a number of novels, many of which, including *Count Julian*, *Makbara*, *The Blind Rider*, and *Quarantine*, have been translated into English.

PETER BUSH has translated nine books by Juan Goytisolo including his autobiography and his novels *Quarantine* and *The Marx Family Saga*, which won the Ramón Valle-Inclán Prize for Literary Translation, as well as novels by Nuria Amat, Fernando de Rojas, Juan Carlos Onetti, Leonardo Padura, and other prominent Spanish and Latin American writers.

COLEMAN DOWELL SERIES

The Coleman Dowell Series is made possible through a generous contribution by an anonymous donor. This endowed contribution allows Dalkey Archive Press to publish one book a year in this series.

Born in Kentucky in 1925, Coleman Dowell moved to New York in 1950 to work in theater and television as a playwright and composer/lyricist, but by age forty he turned to writing fiction. His works include *One of the Children Is Crying* (1968), *Mrs. October Was Here* (1974), *Island People* (1976), *Too Much Flesh and Jabez* (1977), and *White on Black on White* (1983). After his death in 1985, *The Houses of Children: Collected Stories* was published in 1987, and his memoir about his theatrical years, *A Star-Bright Lie*, was published in 1993.

Since his death, a number of his books have been reissued in the United States, as well as translated for publication in other countries.

SELECTED DALKEY ARCHIVE PAPERBACKS

FOR A FULL LIST OF PUBLICATIONS, VISIT:

www.dalkeyarchive.com

SELECTED DALKEY ARCHIVE PAPERBACKS

FOR A FULL LIST OF PUBLICATIONS, VISIT:

www.dalkeyarchive.com